THE LAST BOUNTY

Jack Sutcliffe knew he would have trouble getting Bart Durrant up to Fort Smith so that they could hang him. Meeting up with the Morris brothers got things off to a bad start. Then Jenny was raped and she came after them all, looking for revenge. As if that wasn't bad enough, a second bounty hunter set out to hijack Durrant. The lead soon began to fly and Jack Sutcliffe's last bounty was destined to end in a bloody shoot-out.

Books by H. H. Cody
in the Linford Western Library:

LAST STOP ON THE TRAIL

Doncaster
Metropolitan Borough Council

DONCASTER LIBRARY AND INFORMATION SERVICES

Please return/renew this item by the last date shown.
Thank you for using your library.

H. H. CODY

THE LAST BOUNTY

Complete and Unabridged

LINFORD
Leicester

First published in Great Britain in 1998 by
Robert Hale Limited
London

First Linford Edition
published 1999
by arrangement with
Robert Hale Limited
London

The moral right of the author
has been asserted

British Library CIP Data

Cody, H. H.
    The last bounty.—Large print ed.—
Linford western library
1. Western stories
2. Large type books
I. Title
823.9′14 [F]

ISBN 0–7089–5568–1

Published by
F. A. Thorpe (Publishing) Ltd.
Anstey, Leicestershire

Set by Words & Graphics Ltd.
Anstey, Leicestershire
Printed and bound in Great Britain by
T. J. International Ltd., Padstow, Cornwall

This book is printed on acid-free paper

1

'OK, now git up, you ain't hurt.' Jack Sutcliffe stood over his quarry who lay in the dirt, his yellow eyes ablaze with anger, blood already drying among the stubble that furred the animal slyness of Bart Durrant's face.

As Durrant moved to get up, Sutcliffe drew back his foot and crashed it into Durrant's ribs. With a cry of pain and rage, the outlaw fell back into the dust. He writhed. Holding his ribs, he tried slowly to roll to where his gun lay. Sutcliffe saw what his aim was and moved quickly to head it off. His booted foot stood on the pistol as Durrant's hand reached for it. Then, Sutcliffe stamped on the outlaw's fingers.

'Bastard,' spat out Durrant. 'You won't live to collect yer blood money, that's fer sure.'

Sutcliffe, a tall rangy man dressed in a blue shirt and blue trousers, wearing a tied-down Peacemaker, spat into the ground, then picked up Durrant's pistol and stuck it in his own belt. Grabbing Durrant by the collar, he hauled him to his feet and pushed him towards his horse.

'I've come a long way not to get to live to spend that bounty they got on you, you miserable son-of-a-bitch. And I'm gonna see Judge Parker hangs you,' Sutcliffe said with less confidence than he felt. He knew that Bart Durrant's gang were somewhere in the area.

By a piece of luck, he'd got Durrant just where he wanted him, but he could bet that Durrant's boys were going to do their damnedest to see that their boss kept his head out of a noose.

For years the Durrant gang had been running in and out of Indian Territory, making a name for themselves robbing banks and stages, doing almost anything they pleased, but Bart Durrant had a weakness, and that weakness was women. One woman in particular: a squaw named Running Deer who lived with her family up in the Territory. Every now and then, Durrant would mosey up to the Territory to see her for a spell. Sutcliffe got to know about this and spread some *dinero* around. It paid off. Word had got down to him at Ryker's Post that Durrant was visiting Running Deer. Immediately, Sutcliffe got himself out of the bed of the soiled dove with whom he had been sporting the night and lit out. He'd arrived ten minutes after Durrant had left to put miles between him and his squaw. The trail had not been hard to follow.

Eventually, Durrant came into sight. The desperation in Sutcliffe's loins transmitted itself to his mount and soon he overhauled Durrant, dragged him out of the saddle and beat him into submission.

Planting the sole of his boot in Durrant's rear end, he gave him one extra push of encouragement. Durrant went spinning away, still holding his ribs. Latching on to the horn he tried to pull himself up into the saddle.

'Cain't y'give me a hand?' The pain forced him to screw up his face.

'You either get yer ass in that saddle or you walk to yer hangin'. Make up your mind an' make it up quick. Don't like to keep Judge Parker waitin'.'

Pulling his own gun, Sutcliffe drew back the hammer and fired a shot into the dirt. Durrant made one more attempt to get into the saddle. This time he made it.

'Smart move.' Sutcliffe walked round to his horse and mounted up. He had no fear of Durrant making a break for it; he was as good a shot with a Winchester as he was with a Peacemaker.

With Durrant still holding his sides, they moved out of the shallow canyon, Sutcliffe keeping his eyes on the outlaw every second. Durrant was a cunning and cruel man, who would stop at nothing to get what he wanted. And Sutcliffe knew that he was not going to have an easy task getting him to Fort Smith so that Judge Isaac Parker could hang him.

The country flattened out and, in the distance, Sutcliffe could make out the trading post where he knew that he could get some grub before heading out. There had been no time to do anything but check his guns before going after Durrant.

'OK, hold it there,' he called out to Durrant, as they entered the yard of the post. Durrant hauled on the leathers.

'You sure soon had enough,' the outlaw sneered, turning to give Sutcliffe a vicious smile.

'Just want to make it plain, so there's no mistake. We're pullin' in at the post for some eats. Try anythin' smart an' you'll git a bullet in yer sorry ass. Got that?' He drew up close to Durrant and grabbed him by the shirt front, twisting him sideways so that they were looking face to face.

A fierce hatred burned deep in Durrant's yellow eyes. 'Like I said,

5

you got to get me back first, Sutcliffe. You'd just better pray I don't get you in the kinda mess I'm in.'

'Just hold yer mouth an' ride down there,' Sutcliffe replied, and gigged his horse in the direction of the post.

It looked unimpressive to anyone coming into it. It was a low building with a couple of rudely built corrals which held the horses of those who used the post in their various dealings — legal or otherwise.

White Elk, the woman of Sol Greer who ran the post, stood just outside the door tossing corn to a bunch of scrawny chickens that were fighting for the food and didn't look as though they'd make a decent mouthful for a starving wolf. Seeing the two riders approaching, she put the shallow basket down on the ground and disappeared inside.

Sutcliffe climbed down from his horse and hitched it to the lopsided rail. For a moment, he looked around, then, satisfied that everything was in order, he dragged Durrant from his horse.

'Keep still an' don't try anything,' Sutcliffe told him as he took a rope from his saddle. Cutting a length, he tied Durrant's hands to the hitch rail.

'There's food inside if that's what you want.' White Elk had come out and was standing with her hands on her hips. 'Got other things as well,' she said, with a broad smile, pretending not to recognize Durrant.

'No, the food'll do,' Sutcliffe told her.

'What about him?' White Elk gestured to Durrant.

'Feed him if y'want,' Sutcliffe answered without turning round. 'I'll pay for it. Anything else comes out of his own pocket.' He heard the squaw laugh as he went in.

At first, it was hard to see much of the inside of the post. To his left, stood a long bar with shelves behind it packed with goods of all kinds. Crowded in the middle of the room were four tables. Three of them were empty. Two men sat at the fourth table, dressed in shabby range clothes, with glasses in front of them and a bottle, half-empty, in the middle. The one with his back to Sutcliffe turned at his partner's word.

Ignoring them, Sutcliffe went to the counter.

'What'll it be?' Sol Greer stood behind the counter, folding up the month-old newspaper and putting it out of sight.

Sutcliffe tipped back his hat and leaned on the counter. 'Beer. And whatever else there is to eat.' He ran his hand over his face to take away the sweat, waiting while the fat man filled a beer glass. There was no conversation in the place, only the steady humming of the hungry flies that swarmed above the tables. Greer came back with Sutcliffe's beer and set it down.

'Just go an' see how long yer food's gonna be. Potatoes an' steak OK?'

Greer asked without any enthusiasm.

'If that's all there is.' Sutcliffe took up the glass and put it to his mouth. It didn't taste like the best beer in the world, but it cleaned the dust out of his mouth and throat.

'Be about fifteen minutes,' Greer said, reaching for the newspaper.

'That'll be fine.' Sutcliffe raised the glass to his mouth and drained it. 'Mind fixin' me another?'

'Sure thing, Mr Sutcliffe.' Greer reached for the glass.

A look of recognition at the mention of Sutcliffe's name crossed the faces of the men behind the bounty hunter.

'You Jack Sutcliffe, the bounty hunter?' one of the men asked, turning slowly in his chair.

'Yeah, I'm Jack Sutcliffe,' Sutcliffe said, half turning. 'Now, how about that beer?' Sutcliffe turned back to Greer, pushing the empty glass towards him.

Behind him, Sutcliffe heard a sudden restless stirring. His mind became alert, his hand falling to his gun, but the noise settled down. Greer put a second glass in front of Sutcliffe who took it to the back of the room, conscious of the veiled looks of the men at the table. Sutcliffe sat with his back to the wall.

A moment later, White Elk entered and went straight through to the back room. Sutcliffe yawned. The room had suddenly become even hotter and days on the trail with no proper sleep began to make themselves felt. Across the room, a chair scraped as it was pushed away from the table.

Sutcliffe felt the tension in his neck. He hit the floor a split second before a bullet sliced the air where his head had been. As he fell sideways, his own gun came out, the hammer back.

The two men had split up, one on either side of him. The one on his left had framed himself in the doorway, his gun spitting for a second chance, but his view had been blocked by a table in front of him. His shot went wide and Sutcliffe fired between the tables.

He heard a scream and the man fell, clutching his shin.

There was just time to turn his attention to the second man who had kicked a chair out of his way. Sutcliffe fired over the top of the table and into the body of the man, who screamed and spun backwards, blood spurting from the hole in his chest. He staggered back against the counter where he hung for a moment, then slid to the floor.

Kicking a chair out of the way, Sutcliffe trained his gun on the man who was clutching at his smashed shin, the blood running through his fingers.

'Just don't shoot me, please,' he whined, as Sutcliffe advanced on him purposefully. For a moment, complete silence descended on the room as the black gunsmoke drifted towards a window and Sutcliffe thought about it. The air hung heavy with the smell of blood and death.

Sutcliffe dropped the gun back into its holster after making sure that the wounded man could not reach his own gun.

'Hell, why would I do that?' he asked, dropping down to pull the man's hand from his wound.

'Leg's a mess. Gonna be walking on crutches for a spell,' he said conversationally, pulling a crushed cheroot from his vest pocket. Straightening it out, he pulled a match across the floor. He put the flame to the end of the cheroot and blew smoke in the wounded man's direction. The man coughed and spluttered.

'OK, friend, who are you?' Sutcliffe asked, pulling on the cheroot.

'I'm Buz Hardin,' he ground out through clenched teeth.

Sutcliffe threw a nod in the direction of the dead man. 'He have a name?'

'His name wuz Al Watkins. We did some bounty huntin' along the Brazos an' came up here fer a change. We heard you and the fella behind the bar talkin' an' . . . an' . . . ' He winced with pain.

12

'An' you figgered you'd save me the trouble of takin' him in.' Sutcliffe took the cheroot out of his mouth and pushed it into Hardin's. 'Enjoy the smoke.'

He stood up. Hardin's eyes followed him with a little less certainty than they had contained a moment before. Hardin was wondering if Sutcliffe had changed his mind about not shooting him.

'If'n I clap eyes on you again, yer a dead man.' Sutcliffe returned to the counter. 'That food ready yet?'

'Sure. Yeah,' Greer babbled, his face a lot more pasty than it had been a while back.

As Sutcliffe ate, a couple of men appeared from out back and started to clean up the mess. For a moment, the bounty hunter watched them, then went outside to where Durrant waited, still attached to the hitch-rail. He was being fed by the squaw. He saw the disappointment in Durrant's face when he appeared.

'Sorry if you got yer hopes up, but it just didn't pan out for them new boys,' he told him.

'No disappointment to me. Sooner do it myself. Long way to Judge Parker's court an' I'm gittin' a real itch to see you roast over a good hot fire.' Durrant hawked and spat.

'You keep on itchin'; it's gonna be scratched raw by the time we get up there.' Sutcliffe went back inside, leaving the squaw to finish feeding Durrant.

'You remember, White Elk. Soon as me an' Sutcliffe is clear of here, you git word to Running Deer. She'll bring the boys. You know which way we're goin'.'

'Minute you and Sutcliffe leave, I will be on my way,' she said, shovelling another forkful of pork into Durrant's mouth.

Sutcliffe ate quickly, anxious to be on his way in case anybody else wanted to relieve him of his prisoner. He gave Greer payment for the meal and went outside. White Elk was wiping Durrant's face with a cloth. She took his plate and scurried inside when she saw Sutcliffe, who wondered why she had hurried away, but did not stop to find out. Instead, he unfastened Durrant from the hitch-rail and told him to get mounted. They pulled out of the yard and headed for Fort Smith.

2

As Sutcliffe and Durrant made their way out of the yard, Sol Greer came to the door and watched them for a few minutes. Presently, he was joined by White Elk.

'You reckon your sister's gonna be comin' fer Durrant?' he asked her.

'She will be coming for the white snake in the grass, for she loves him.' White Elk sounded surprised at the question.

For many years she had lived with the white man. Occasionally he made love to her and between them they had five children. The whites could be both good and bad, like her own people, but she could not understand why a good woman like her sister chose to offer her sleeping blanket to a man like Durrant, a man who did not love her and who only used her when he was nearby. But,

16

Running Deer was her sister and if she needed help, White Elk would give it.

'Now, you git yourself a horse. Take that palomino. Al Watkins won't be having no use fer him now,' Greer said. 'Git word to your sister that Sutcliffe's on his way to Fort Smith. Tell her to git Somers and the boys. But be careful, it's Jack Sutcliffe they'll be goin' up against.'

He watched as White Elk went to the barn to come out again a few minutes later leading the palomino that had once belonged to Al Watkins. Getting mounted, the squaw rode out of the trading post in the opposite direction to that taken by Sutcliffe and his prisoner.

Buz Hardin had passed out and come to again by the time White Elk had mounted the palomino. Greer's men had put him in the dark back room, musty with the fetid air of food going stale.

'How are y' feelin'?' Greer asked, when he came in. Not that he had to

17

be told. Holding the lamp high in his hand, he bent over Hardin's body. The colour had gone from the flesh, leaving him looking pale and half dead.

'How do you think I feel?' Hardin asked harshly. 'Pretty lousy. Damned bounty hunter did fer Al an' damn near did fer me.'

'You just weren't quick enough, that's all,' Greer said mournfully. 'There's always another day.' He watched Hardin's face carefully. Sure enough, he thought, it's beginning to grow. Soon as Hardin's fit enough to ride, he'll go looking for Sutcliffe and put a bullet in his bounty-hunting hide.

'You bet there's another day,' said Hardin, as he stared fixedly into the dark. He winced and clutched at his leg.

★ ★ ★

While Greer and Buz Hardin were swapping talk in the back room,

18

Sutcliffe had started to give some thought to a camp for the night. Now, with the sun starting to fall into the west behind the hills, his eyes located a stand of cottonwoods about half a mile away.

'This is as far as we're goin' fer today,' the bounty hunter said.

When they got to the trees, Sutcliffe led them slowly along a narrow, winding trail until they came to a clearing.

Sutcliffe hauled the outlaw out of the saddle.

'Gonna leave this on 'til we git to Fort Smith?' Durrant asked.

'No. Even I'm human enough to know that when a man's gotta go, he's gotta go.' Sutcliffe reached behind him and took a hunting knife from his belt. 'Hold still.'

The blade cut through the ropes and freed Durrant, who immediately rubbed his wrists to get the circulation going.

'Thank ye, kindly, Mister Bounty

19

Hunter, sir.' He gave Sutcliffe a mock bow.

'There's some wood just behind you; git a fire goin'.' Sutcliffe put the knife away and pulled out his Peacemaker.

It did not take Durrant long to get the wood and turn it into a cookfire. Sutcliffe tossed him bacon from his saddle-bag, along with coffee then he handed him a canteen.

'It's all yours,' he said, as Durrant caught the stuff.

Half an hour later, he said, 'You've missed yer callin', my dishonest friend. Cooking's more in your line.' He licked his fingers clean and tossed the plate across to Durrant to wash.

Durrant hunkered down when the stuff was put away.

'Gonna tie you up again.' Sutcliffe took the rope from his saddle horn and cut another long piece. He bound Durrant's hands tightly at the back of the man.

'Tell me, Sutcliffe, what rides a man like you to track his own kind down fer the money?' Durrant asked.

'Your kind does,' Sutcliffe told him. 'I come from a place where there was no law. My old man took a bullet trying to stop scum like you cleanin' out a bank.'

'More fool him. Shoulda let it go. Money's no use to you if yer dead.' Durrant stretched in front of the fire and wriggled until he had got himself comfortable.

'He didn't see it that way.' Sutcliffe, who had unsaddled the horses, laid his head against his saddle and pulled his hat down over his eyes. It did not take him long to fall into a light sleep.

The dream came back. A red-hot day in the small town of Gila Springs. Three men dressed in long jackets ride slowly up the main street. They stop outside the bank. Two get down and go inside. The third holds the reins for the others. Frank Sutcliffe comes out of the store just as the shooting starts inside the bank. Seconds later, the two men come tumbling out, firing wildly. The street fills up, and among the onlookers are children. Frank grabs a Winchester from a buckboard and levers a round into the chamber. As he brings it up to his shoulder, the bank robber who holds the reins cuts him down with a bullet from his 45, laughing wildly as he does so. The others get in their saddles and ride out of town before anybody can do anything to stop them.

Sutcliffe woke with a start. By the dying embers of the fire he could make out Durrant sleeping soundly, like a newborn babe. For a moment, he regarded the outlaw with a savage hatred. It had been someone like Bart Durrant who had gunned down his pa.

The fire moved and the embers fell in on themselves sending up a red shower to the clear night sky. Sutcliffe watched the sky for a moment and closed his eyes, but he knew that he would not sleep again. He tried to relax himself and wait out the night.

Durrant woke just after sun-up. To him it was obvious that Sutcliffe had not slept; he had heard him moving about. The thought made him smile. A tired man was a careless man.

'Come on, move yourself,' Jack Sutcliffe came out from behind a tree where he had been relieving himself. Durrant pretended to yawn and stretch then he got slowly to his feet.

'Damn fine night's sleep,' he said, with a sly grin at Sutcliffe. 'Mornin' like this makes a man feel good to be alive.'

'Glad you see it that way. Ain't gonna be many more,' the bounty hunter replied callously.

Sutcliffe cut the bonds that held Durrant's hands together.

'Fix some coffee an' grub. Want to be on the trail pretty soon.' Sutcliffe eyed Durrant as he blew on the embers of the fire to get a blaze going. Bastard's up to something, but what? he thought to himself.

Durrant fixed breakfast and served it

23

up without any kind of complaint or bad word. When he had finished he began to whistle.

When Durrant was all through, Sutcliffe made him saddle up. Then he retied his hands, then saddled his own horse.

'Let's be moving,' he called out.

★ ★ ★

White Elk took hold of the horse's mane and swung herself up on to its bare back. Greer watched her ride out of the yard and gave her a wave. He knew that she would be gone until the following day, which meant that he and his latest woman, who lived in a cabin behind the post, would have plenty of time to themselves. It would take White Elk several hours to reach Running Deer's village. Until White Elk had met Sol Greer when he had come to her village to trade with her father, the sisters had been inseparable. Greer had returned several times and each time had shown a growing interest in White Elk. Finally, a dowry had been agreed between them, and when Red Eagle, White Elk's pa, accepted the five horses and numerous other presents, White Elk had returned to the post as Greer's wife. She had not been happy or unhappy as Sol Greer's wife, simply accepting her lot. Yet she envied Running Deer her life in the village and her comparative freedom. Greer was a kind man, but he did not fully understand the red men and their ways.

Years of child-bearing had thickened her once slim waist, and she sometimes wondered if her husband took his pleasure with some of the white women who lived around the post.

The tent of Running Deer's father stood in the centre of the village. A few of the tribe were about and when one of them saw her coming, they fetched Running Deer to greet her sister.

'What brings you to our village?' Running Deer asked, in a tone that suggested to White Elk that she might already have guessed why.

'The white bounty man, Sutcliffe, has captured your man and is taking him to Fort Smith to face Judge Parker,' White Elk gabbled out as soon as she had got down from the horse.

A troubled look crossed Running Deer's face. She knew that Judge Parker would hang her man for his crimes against the white-man's laws. Her love for Durrant was great and it would kill her if the white man's judge hanged him. She had to help him.

'What thought turns in that mind of yours, my daughter?' Neither of the women had heard Red Eagle emerge from the tepee behind them. Although not a big man, Red Eagle's bearing and nobility gave the impression of him being a lot taller than he was. 'I have heard the news your sister has brought and know how unhappy it must make you.'

'I must help the man that I love,'

Running Deer said simply.

Red Eagle's face hardened when he heard his daughter's words. He knew that he would not ask any of his braves to help his daughter. If she went she would have to go alone.

As if reading his thoughts, Running Deer said, 'I know that my father does not like the man that I have chosen and he will not have him in our lodge. When he visits me we must make a lodge outside the village.' She hesitated, realizing that she had reached the point where she must make a choice between her father and the man she loved. 'I will take my own horse and, with your permission, a rifle and ammunition. There are those who will help us.'

White Elk knew that her sister was talking about the Durrant gang, holed up a couple of miles away, probably wondering what had become of their boss.

'Very well, my daughter, if that is your choice,' Red Eagle spoke gravely.

'My lodge will always be open to you. You alone.'

Having said her farewells, Running Deer and her father took their leave of one another. Red Eagle watched his daughter go with a heavy heart, but he too had a decision to make and, as much as it grieved him to say farewell to his daughter in these circumstances, he had the welfare of his tribe to consider.

The two women mounted their ponies and cantered to the head of the valley. With a heavy heart, Running Deer turned to look back once and raised the rifle in salute.

★ ★ ★

Durrant's wrists were sore as hell with the binding that Sutcliffe had put on them. For an hour or so they had been riding without a word passing between them. He wondered how long it would be before Sutcliffe needed some rest, but for now the bounty hunter seemed to be doing just fine.

'What y'goin' to do with the money you git fer me, allowin' you make it to Fort Smith?' he called over his shoulder.

Sutcliffe watched him closely for a moment before answering. Bart Durrant had not made any conversation since they had set out that morning, so what was going through his mind now, Sutcliffe wondered. Maybe he had the idea that he could get under Sutcliffe's skin and make him angry enough to do something stupid.

'Fixin' to git you a better headstone than you deserve,' he called back harshly.

The words seemed to have no effect on the outlaw, who shrugged them off. The silence fell once again between the two men. Sutcliffe regarded Durrant. Durrant had started young. As a kid he'd beaten up other kids and taken what few coins they had or anything else that he had fancied. From there, he'd graduated to robbing banks and stage-coaches, along with a train or two. Now, he was set for a rope.

His last job, with his gang, had involved a rancher who owned a lot of cattle and cash. To get at the cash, Durrant had figured that the rancher would do a deal if they kidnapped his wife, which is what they did. Things went a little wrong, however, and the rancher's wife had been killed. That was when the heat was turned up on the gang, and when Sutcliffe decided to go after him. The bounty on Durrant had gone up to $5,000. His *segundo*, Rick Mellors, rated $3,000.

3

It was not much of a town, hardly a town at all, just a collection of badly built buildings. There was a saloon, a whorehouse and a general store, along with a parcel of houses that had been built around the place. Drifting trade kept it going, travellers going further West, men and women on the run, those just trying to disappear. Durrant and his gang used it when Durrant felt the urge to visit Running Deer. They stayed a couple of days, getting liquored up and giving the soiled doves in the whorehouse some more to spend.

As the best room in the place it was still a mess. The paint on the walls was peeling like the skin on a man whom the Apaches had had their hands on. The window that looked out over the back alley needed cleaning so badly that it was a chore to tell whether it was night or day.

Rick Mellors got up from his chair and stalked around the room. The air was foul with smoke and the smell of stale whiskey and the cheap perfume in which the whores doused themselves when they came from the whorehouse across the street.

Mellors was a thickset bull of a man, with long bushy eyebrows that met over the top of his hawk nose.

'What's bitin' you?' Pete Somers asked, from the bed in the corner of the room.

'Where the boss is, is what's bitin' me,' Mellors scowled dangerously. 'Shoulda bin back by now. Never takes him this long,' he added.

'Maybe his squaw wanted somethin' unusual,' Somers went on. 'Know how these Indian women can be.'

Mellors flared up angrily and grabbed Somers by the shirt front, dragging him off the bed.

'Best not let him catch you talkin'

about his woman like that.' Mellors let go of the shirt front and Somers fell to the floor. The whores in the room squealed, then got back against the wall out of the way.

'Hey, we didn't come over here to get caught up in this,' Rita Harris, the madam from the whore-house complained, wiping down the front of her pink dress with her hands.

Mellors had caught the edge of the table when he had let go of Somers and tipped over a glass of beer that had gone all over the blonde.

'Shut yer damn mouth,' he stormed, raising his hand to strike her and causing her to press herself further against the wall, her face paling under her paint.

'Gonna cost you a heap extra for that, Mellors. This dress came out by stage from New York. It didn't come cheap,' she stormed, her blue eyes shining like chips of ice. She remembered how pleased she had been on opening the mail packet that Durrant and Somers had tossed on to the table, and on seeing the New York address on the brown paper parcel that she had torn open, her ecstasy on seeing the dress and Somers telling her that she could have it.

'I know it didn't come cheap. Near took a bullet from the shot-gun guard gettin' it fer you,' he reminded her angrily.

'This ain't gettin' us nowhere,' Three Fingers Harkins said, as he fiddled with a piece of string. Despite the handicap of three fingers of his right hand having been blown off when some dynamite that he had fixed to a safe went up prematurely, he managed it pretty well.

'What'd you mean?' The fourth member of the Durrant gang hauled himself back to reality. Willy Brown had a sly face that matched his sly thoughts.

Sighing heavily, Mellors rolled up his eyes at the flaking ceiling. 'Means we're thinkin' o' goin' lookin' fer Bart.

Should've been back from seein' his woman before now.'

'Oh,' Willy said, after some thought. 'Mean we ain't gonna be stayin' here a spell longer with these pretty ladies?'

'Means just that.' Mellors threw himself down on the bed next to Somers, then got up suddenly, as if bored with the whole thing. 'We'll go an' look for Bart.'

'How we know where he's gonna be?' Willy asked.

'Know where he's been. Know where he's comin from, know which trail he's gonna be usin',' Mellors said patiently.

'Oh yeah,' said a finally satisfied Willy.

'When are you gonna be leavin'?' Rita gave them a long look as she figured out how much she and her girls could wring out of them before they left.

'Reckon it's gonna have to be first light.' Rick Mellors went to the window. 'Too late to start now.' He

35

reached for the whiskey bottle and put it to his mouth.

With a feeling of satisfaction, Rita went to tell the girls they had another night's work in front of them.

★ ★ ★

They were lying low in the undergrowth. Sutcliffe had drawn his revolver, his cold, blue eyes watching the trail ahead of him. He did not know what had made him haul off the trail and pull a startled Durrant out of the saddle and clap his hand over Durrant's mouth.

He eased his hand away. 'There's riders comin' this way,' he told his prisoner. 'And I want to be sure I know who they are before I let them know we're here.'

They were masked from the trail by thick brush that poked at their faces and scratched at their eyes. No sound came from up ahead, only the feeling in Sutcliffe's neck that whoever was up ahead was not far away.

The blow fell on Sutcliffe's head and everything exploded in a shower of bright lights. The Peacemaker fell from his grasp as he pitched forward.

It was dark when he came to. Durrant lay next to him, still bound hand and foot. As Sutcliffe tried to move, he found that he too had been tied up, the ropes burning wickedly into the flesh of his wrists. In the middle of the clearing, a strong fire burned throwing bright light on the three men who sat around it eating beans and drinking the coffee that he could smell. The men were talking in low tones, laughing occasionally. One of them, a bear of a man who seemed to be the leader, got up and walked to where he had left his saddle. From a saddle-bag he pulled out a bottle of whiskey. Glancing over to where Sutcliffe lay, he saw that the bounty man was watching him.

'Hold this, Ben,' he said, handing the bottle to one of his companions.

As soon as he called the name, Sutcliffe recognized him. That meant that the other men around the camp-fire were Fred Morris's brothers, Homer and Ben. Inwardly, Sutcliffe cursed, he did not want to believe what he had seen or heard.

For two months he had chased the Morris gang at a time when there had been four of them. He had done for John Morris in a burning saloon. Trapped inside it, John would not surrender, so Sutcliffe went in after him. A brief gunfight had followed with John stopping a bullet in the chest. Before Sutcliffe could get to him, fire had raged through the wooden building devouring it in no time at all.

John had died screaming in the flames.

Homer got his hands under Jack Sutcliffe's armpits and pulled him towards the fire. The others watched.

Ben pulled the cork out of the bottle and spat it into the fire. 'Well, howdy, Jack,' he said cheerfully, as Homer dumped his bundle on the ground. 'Bin looking forward to this fer quite a spell. Got a few things to talk over with you. That so, boys?'

'Sure as hell is,' the others put in, like an out-of-tune choir.

'Talkin' about our brother on the trail up here. Runnin' into Greer sure as hell made our day.' He tilted the bottle back and swallowed. Homer snatched the whiskey from his hand before it was all gone.

It went quiet for a while as they passed it around. At length, Homer looked across at Durrant who was watching it all in silence, wondering what was going to happen to him and if he could get out of the mess.

Homer caught his look. 'Don't worry, when yer time comes it's gonna be a hell of a sight quicker than his is gonna be.'

'That'd be a joke, wouldn't it?' Ben put in, throwing a glance Durrant's way.

'What's that, Brother?' Fred asked, his voice sounding as though the effects of the whiskey were getting to him.

'Be the hell of a joke to ride into Fort

Smith with him, collect the reward an' tell them that he killed Sutcliffe here. 'Course we couldn't take ol' Sutcliffe's body in as there isn't gonna be much left to take in.'

The laugh of the men chilled Sutcliffe's bones.

While this was going on, Homer got to his feet and went behind Sutcliffe, who was suddenly reminded of his presence when a boot thudded into his back. The pain tore through the bounty-man's body, so much so that he arched upwards. The other two roared with laughter. Homer, truly into his stride, grabbed Sutcliffe and pushed him through the fire. Emerging at the other side, Ben's hands caught him, spun him round and pushed him through the flames again.

The flames licked at Sutcliffe's hands and face as he went through them. Fred held him then slammed his fist into him. Sutcliffe felt his ribs start to ache under the pummelling.

'Go easy on him, now,' he heard Ben

call out to the others. 'Don't want the fun ending too soon.'

Sutcliffe felt himself thrown to the ground with the wind knocked out of his body. The taste of his own blood was bitter in his mouth.

'He can take some more before we rest him,' laughed Homer.

The time that followed blurred into the dark of the night as the fists slammed into Sutcliffe's body and face. One of his eyes closed completely. His body felt as though somebody had run a herd of buffalo over it. And still they showed no sign of letting up. The world spun round until it finally disappeared into the dark.

'You sure look a mess,' Sutcliffe heard the voice of Bart Durrant coming at him out of the dark.

He tried to speak but his whole face and mouth were too swollen and thick for him to get anything out.

'Yeah, a real mess.' A tone of satisfaction had crept into Durrant's voice. 'An' the way I figure it, you got some more comin'.'

Sutcliffe rolled over on to his back. From what he could see out of his one eye, the three men were enjoying their breakfast, casting an occasional glance at him. A pot of coffee was being passed round.

Ben came over to him with a canteen in his hand. Taking off the cap he held it to Sutcliffe's swollen lips and poured the water into his mouth. Sutcliffe coughed and gagged.

'Don't want y' dying on us yet awhile,' he laughed cruelly, striking Sutcliffe's back.

The mouthful of water perked Sutcliffe up more than he would have thought possible. Ben Morris then stood over Bart Durrant with the canteen in his hand.

'Cost you five hundred dollars for a mouthful. But I reckon you ain't got that kinda money on you, have you?' He tipped the canteen so that the water spilled into the ground.

'I ain't got five cents on me.' The

42

tone of his voice made Ben stop pouring the water away.

'You're interestin', but you'd better keep bein' interestin'. Otherwise it's gonna take you the hell of a long time to die. Savvy?'

'I savvy. Know where I can lay my hands on a lot more than that.' Durrant's eyes had never left the canteen. He knew that as well as talking for a mouthful of water he was talking for his life.

'An' just where would this pot o' gold be?' Ben put the top back on the canteen.

'Don't talk so good with a dry mouth,' Durrant said.

Ben pulled the top off again and bent down over the outlaw, allowing the water to run into his mouth. Then he pulled the canteen away.

'Had yer money's worth,' he said, standing up. 'Gonna talk with muh brothers, see what they say. If they're for it, fine; if not, you git what he's gonna git.'

4

Ben Morris walked over to where his brothers were standing by the remains of their breakfast and the fire.

'This here Durrant's got a proposition for us,' he told them.

Homer stopped picking his teeth with a piece of twig.

'What kinda proposition?' He spat out a piece of his breakfast that had lodged in his tooth.

'Reckons he can lay his hands on a heap o' dough.' Ben hunkered down and the others followed suit.

'Cain't see it meself. Don't recall Durrant pullin' anythin' that big,' Fred threw in his two-cents' worth.

'Seems like he's playin' for time.' Homer picked himself another piece of twig and went at his teeth again.

'Dunno,' Ben said. 'They pulled a fair number of jobs, might be all stashed away in one place.'

'Might at that,' Fred said slowly, like it was a big effort. 'Couldn't have spent all that *dinero*.'

'So what do we do about it?' Ben asked, looking from one to the other of his brothers. 'Put a bullet in him?'

'No, see if he can come up with the money, then put a bullet in him,' Homer laughed.

Sutcliffe lay watching the discussions, his body still burning from the beating he had taken. He knew that his fate might be decided in the next few minutes.

'What about the bounty man? He's deserving of a bullet by my reckoning.' Homer looked in Sutcliffe's direction as he spoke.

'We gonna draw lots fer it, or does he git one from each of us?' Fred loosened the pistol in his holster.

'One from each of us.' Ben's voice had a tone of finality in it. 'That should do it fer him.'

A cold feeling crawled up Sutcliffe's

belly as he watched the three men coming his way.

'OK,' Homer said to Durrant. 'We thought about it. You just show us where the money is then you ride out. We got no beef with you.'

'Seemed like a set of boys who'd see sense,' Durrant smiled ingratiatingly.

'Now, where'd you say it wuz?' Ben asked, getting up close to Durrant.

'Sure, I tell you that an' I ain't got a card in my hand,' he said with a thoughtful frown.

'Can see the sense of that,' Ben went on. 'But yer gonna have to give us a couple of hints like.'

'Waal.' Durrant thought hard. 'All I'm gonna tell you is that it's within spittin' distance of Fort Smith. Then we'll talk about how we go our separate ways without me gittin' a bullet off you fellas.'

The three men snorted loudly. 'Hell,' Homer said, pulling his piece. 'Might as well shoot him now.'

'Reckon so,' Ben horned in. 'We ain't

gonna git near that place. Our faces are well known round Fort Smith.'

Sutcliffe, who had been listening intently, saw his chance.

'They know me too,' he put in, watching the faces of the men whose brother he had shot. He was figuring the longer he stayed alive the greater were his chances of getting out of this mess.

Homer's boot swung into his ribs. 'Stay outa this, bounty man, or yer'll make it that much worse for yerself.'

'What do ya mean?' Fred put in.

'If anybody sees you riding with me they won't think nothin' of it. See you on yer own with him, they might think different.'

'Might at that,' Ben replied thoughtfully. 'Yeah, might just work at that.'

Homer grabbed Sutcliffe by his shirt front. Sutcliffe came up so suddenly that the earth spun and the pain in his ribs and back drove fiery waves through him.

'OK, bounty man, git this an' git it

47

good 'cos I ain't gonna be tellin' you agin. You come along with us. Don't do anything smart an' it'll just be a bullet instead of all those Indian tricks me an' the boys picked up. Savvy?'

'Savvy,' Sutcliffe replied thickly, through the waves of pain.

★ ★ ★

'There is just one place our paths will cross,' Running Deer told White Elk as they rested their ponies on a ridge overlooking a forest.

'Where is that, my sister?' White Elk put the skin water container to her lips and took a long draught from it.

Running Deer pointed to the west where two trails crossed. The spot was well known as a meeting place for representatives of the Five Tribes. Running Deer took the water skin and drank from it. This done, she returned the skin to White Elk and urged her pony down the slope. The pony was a lively one and she had a little trouble controlling it as they went down the slope. Behind her, she could hear White Elk's less sure-footed mount struggling to keep itself from going over.

The thought of what would happen to her man if Sutcliffe got him to Fort Smith drove her on relentlessly. Her hatred for Sutcliffe grew with each stride her pony took. The judge there, Parker, had a frightening reputation as a judge who would show no mercy. She thought of Durrant dangling from a rope, his body twisting on the end of the thick piece of hemp. She thought of the love she bore him, despite his evil ways.

At the bottom of the ridge, she checked the pony's movement with a light touch of her moccassined foot. White Elk caught up with her and halted her pony.

'Why do you not return to Greer?' she asked. 'This is not your fight. You do not feel for Durrant in the same way that I do.' She eased the rifle that she had borrowed from her father and promised herself that she would soon be close enough to use it.

'It is right that we should go on together. We have shared the same lodge and the same father and we should share the same danger.'

Touching her sister's shoulder, Running Deer smiled her thanks and urged her pony on. White Elk followed.

It took them most of the day to travel the distance to where the trails met. White Elk slid down from the back of her mount and inspected the ground. What she saw pleased her. The gang had not yet passed this way. Running Deer joined her. They tethered their horses in the shadow of a stand of trees, then sat by the trail.

For a while nothing happened, then Running Deer caught the faint sound of harness jingling as the horses approached their resting place. She jumped to her feet, White Elk standing just off the trail covering her sister with the rifle.

50

Durrant's gang came gradually into view, an untidy gaggle of horsemen, strung out along the trail.

'If it ain't Running Deer,' Pete Somers called out, as he brought the others to a halt. 'Where's the boss?' he asked, a sudden note of alarm in his voice.

Running Deer eyed the members of the gang. If she had been alone, she would have feared for her life. Her sister and the fact that she was Durrant's woman made her safe.

'Sutcliffe, the bounty hunter, has him,' Running Deer said quickly.

Mellors swore. Anger showed on the faces of Durrant's gang.

'Where's he takin' him?' Somers demanded quickly.

'Fort Smith to face Judge Parker.' Running Deer spat out the words as White Elk emerged from the trees cradling the rifle.

'Which way d'ya reckon they'd be comin'?' asked Mellors, climbing down from his horse. A moment later the others followed suit and formed a circle around the two squaws.

'From the west.' Running Deer pointed to the distant hills. 'Through the great forest.'

'Then we'd better make sure they don't run into any trouble,' Mellors said, with a sly grin to the others.

The rest of the gang growled their agreement.

'They comin' along with us?' Willy Brown spoke up for the first time. Somers' eyes narrowed in Brown's direction. He knew that Brown had a suspicion of women riding with the gang.

'We are coming with you.' Running Deer swung the Winchester on him, her brown eyes narrowing.

Somers took a step forward between them. 'Sure she's comin' along with us,' he told Brown, who had started to look to the others for support.

'Hell, it ain't gonna do no harm to have them along. 'Specially if she can use the Winchester.' Three Fingers' hand caught hold of Brown's in a restraining gesture.

'Knock it off the both of you,' Mellors said to them. 'We got enough of a problem findin' the boss without you two pitchin' into each other all the way down the trail.'

Brown seemed to relent and his disposition eased a mite. He stepped back. 'Guess that's right,' he said. 'Might as well git started.'

One by one, the others followed him as he mounted up.

They moved out in silence, White Elk and Running Deer in the lead. Three Fingers and Brown rode at the back, eating dust.

5

Homer had taken point with Durrant riding behind him, Durrant's hands had been securely tied to the saddle horn. The rawhide thong had started to cut into the flesh, breaking the skin. He had tried a couple of times to loosen the knots, but in the end had given up. Ben Morris, the one who had tied the knots, knew damn well what he was doing, there was just no play in them. He decided to wait for a better opportunity to make a break for it, if the boys didn't catch up with them. And if any of the others spotted him trying to get free, he figured that his trail would come to a sudden end.

He risked a glance over his shoulder. Sutcliffe must be made of iron to take a beating like he had and still be in the saddle. Homer had tied his hands as well, after cleaning up his face with Sutcliffe's bandanna. Now that it was clear of dried blood and trail dust, Durrant could see the swelling, especially around the eyes, where there had been a lot of punishment. All things considered, the bounty man looked as though somebody had let off a stick of dynamite in his face. Yet it still held a look of defiance; so much so that Ben had planted his fist in the bounty-man's ribs before they set out.

★ ★ ★

Behind him, Sutcliffe could hear the increasingly loud laughter of Fred and Ben. He figured they'd got a bottle and were steadily getting through it. By now they were out on the plain, with Fort Smith getting nearer.

Homer threw up his hand to get them to halt. 'Best git Sutcliffe's hands unfastened,' he called out to Fred and Ben. The laughter ceased suddenly.

'Tie his feet under his horse's belly,' he said as he galloped past Sutcliffe.

'Sure thing, big brother,' Fred called out, a heavy slur in his voice.

'Cain't trust you boys within a mile of a bottle.' Homer's angry voice came loud over the prairie, quickly followed by a slap and yelp of surprised pain from Ben as Homer lashed out at him.

'No call fer that, Homer,' yelled Ben, his voice full of grief. ' 'Twas his bottle.'

'You've had yer share,' Homer snapped back at him. 'Now sober yerselves up. Sutcliffe's hell with a gun, beaten raw or not.'

Nursing a swelling face, Ben dragged Sutcliffe off his horse and sliced his bonds with a bone-handled hunting knife. Pushing him back up into the saddle, he fastened his feet together beneath the horse's belly. Then he, too, mounted up.

They moved on in silence, with only the creaking of dry saddle leather and the jingle of harness to break the monotonous silence of the journey.

Before long, noon came and the sun hung directly overhead. The pain in Sutcliffe's bones had eased considerably, moving on to a dull ache. All the time he watched Durrant and the Morris boys.

Suddenly, Homer swung round and headed back towards his brothers.

'Look'ee there,' he sang out. Sutcliffe looked in the direction in which he was pointing. At first, he saw nothing, then just a faint trace of black smoke against the blue sky.

'Just some damn homestead,' Fred said in disgust. 'Don't mean nothin'.'

'Sure does,' Ben told him. 'Means they're gonna have some decent grub fer us.'

'You're sure stupid.' Fred swung his horse's head around.

'How'd you make that out?' Ben asked in surprise.

' 'Cos we ain't got any money,' came the satisfied reply.

'Hell, I never thought of that,' Homer shouted sarcastically to his brother.

'Who said anythin' 'bout payin' fer it?'

'Don't figure yer meanin'.' Fred scratched his head for a moment.

'Got guns, ain't we?' Homer waved his pistol in the air, a look of exasperation on his mean face.

'Yeah, wuzn't thinkin' fer a minute.' Fred's voice became full of meaning.

They moved on until they came to a stand of trees. Then, Homer and his brothers held a quiet conversation that Sutcliffe could not hear.

When they had finished, Homer came across to them and cut Durrant out of the saddle. 'Me an' the brothers are goin' up yonder.' He turned to Sutcliffe. 'You're gonna stay here. Ben, fix him to that tree, then follow us, real slow an' quiet like. Yer comin' too, Durrant, might need an extra gun, though I doubt it.'

'Sure thing, Homer,' Ben cut the hide thong and yanked Sutcliffe who crashed to the ground. He grabbed his hands and tied them behind the bounty-hunter's back.

'Yo' just keep that mouth of yourn shut,' he hissed, holding the knife to Sutcliffe's throat after he had tied him to a tree.

Sutcliffe watched as Ben moved off quietly through the trees following the others.

Durrant saw the place first as he pushed back a branch. The cabin stood in a clearing. Its door was open and a middle-aged man sat on the porch, a pipe in his mouth, a Winchester across his knees. He rocked, his eyes half-closed as the passel of chickens scrabbled among the corn that had been thrown down for them to eat.

'Not much there,' Durrant spoke quietly.

'There.' Homer's voice had thickened with lust as a pretty girl of about twenty came out on to the porch and spoke to the man in the chair.

'Need some more wood fer the stove, Pa.' Her voice was soft and melodious.

'Reckon I'll have to go an' cut

59

some then.' Her father stood up slowly and stretched in the heat of the day. Yawning, he tapped his pipe on the arm of the rocking chair and picked up the axe from the foot of the step.

Suddenly a dog started to bark; a second later it came tearing out of the cabin, its huge jaws slavering, its yellow eyes blazing. It headed straight for the four men.

Durrant heard the man on the step call, 'Yeller, git back here, damn yer worthless hide.' Behind him, the girl had an alarmed look on her face.

For a minute, Homer watched the dog coming towards them. 'Damn it,' he whispered to the others. He raised his pistol to shoot the fast-approaching animal.

Pushing up his hand, Durrant reached behind Homer and took the knife from Homer's sheath. The dog was almost on top of them before he moved. Stepping to one side, he caught the animal under its chin and swung it backwards, cutting short its yelp of surprise. Quickly, the knife flashed as he cut the animal's throat. Blood gushed from the gaping wound, soaking into the hard, dry ground.

The dog twitched and was silent, as Durrant dropped it at his feet. He wiped the blade of the knife on his trouser leg. When he looked up he was staring at Homer's gun, which was an inch from his nose.

'Be real careful when you hand the knife over, or I might fergit we need you.' Homer's eyes were locked on his.

'Sure, Homer.' Durrant turned the knife slowly in his hand and passed it over to Homer.

'Obliged,' Homer said, taking the knife and turning his attention to the cabin.

The four men could hear the man on the veranda calling out to the dog.

'Yeller, damn yer hide,' he repeated, his eyes scanning the undergrowth.

'Gonna have to do somethin',' Fred murmured, as the man came down the wooden steps, his Winchester in his hands. The girl still stood on the steps, her hands raised to shade her eyes as she looked for the dog.

'Yeller,' she called out, as her pa reached the edge of the stand of trees.

The four men had split up, forming a semi-circle around him. Homer, holding the knife he had taken from Durrant, walked towards the man.

As he emerged from the bushes, the man saw him. 'Hey,' he called out, just before Homer buried the knife in his throat. The blood gushed out as the eyes rolled upwards. Homer let him slip to the ground, then held out his hand to take the rifle from him.

'Died real easy,' he said with a grin.

'Let's git some food.' Fred started to hurry forward towards the cabin.

Catching his arm, Homer pulled him back. 'You just take it easy. Don't know who's in there. Fred, you an' Ben work yer way round the other side.' He waved them in the direction of the cabin. They moved out silently.

Durrant could see the girl still standing on the step trying to see the dog.

'This way,' Homer hissed, pulling Durrant in the opposite direction to that which the other two had taken.

'Pa,' the girl called out, with the first traces of fear in her voice. 'Pa, what's goin' on?' she shouted again.

Durrant and Homer had reached the edge of the clearing. It was not more than a few yards across the clearing to the cabin. Watching the girl, Durrant saw her half-turn away from them, her hands still shielding her eyes.

'C'mon,' whispered Homer. The two men raced across the open ground into the shelter of the side of the cabin. The girl had still not seen them or the others.

'Pa,' she called out again, as Homer came from around the side of the building and stepped on to the porch.

'Cain't hear you.' His cruel laugh made the girl turn quickly.

'What do you mean?' she called back to Homer, her face paling as she started to tremble.

'Means he cain't hear you.' The suddenness of Fred's voice caused the girl to start violently and turn to face the two newcomers who had moved up on to the porch when Durrant and Homer showed themselves.

'Git inside,' Ben told her, pushing her towards the door.

'No,' the girl screamed, as the four men crowded round her.

6

Sutcliffe, sitting on the warm grass, had heard the scream of the girl and then silence for a long time. At last he heard someone approaching through the trees. It was Homer.

'Think we'd fergit about you?' he asked, cutting through the rope that held Sutcliffe to the tree.

'Couldn't git that lucky.'

Sutcliffe went in the direction that Homer indicated with his pistol. The door of the cabin was open and he heard a soft, keening wail as he mounted the step.

The cabin was dark and gloomy inside. At first, he could see very little, then, as his eyes grew used to the dark, he could make out the form of a girl sitting on the floor, rocking gently from side to side.

'What've you done to her, you

bastards?' Sutcliffe called out angrily, taking a step forward. Homer's gun struck him behind the ear. Sutcliffe fell forward, half on his hands and knees.

'Git up,' Homer yelled at him.

The other three started laughing. Sutcliffe struggled to his feet, massaging the back of his head.

They hauled him up and tied him to a chair. The girl remained, sobbing quietly, on the floor.

'This here's Jenny. She's a friend of ours,' Homer said, with a thick laugh. 'Don't reckon she's yer sort. But you can have her, if you've a mind.'

Sutcliffe glared at him.

'Kinda think you'd like to have me on the end of yer gun,' Homer said, glaring back at the bounty hunter.

Sutcliffe shook his head. 'Bullets cost money. Kinda like to see you staked out in the sun though. Cheaper, less effort, an' it'd take a damn sight longer fer you to fry.'

'Well, you ain't gonna have that pleasure,' Homer scowled.

'Leave it, Brother,' Ben told him. 'He's jus' tryin' to git you all riled up.'

'Hell,' put in Homer, 'thought the boy was askin' fer another kickin'.'

'Hey, bitch.' Homer grabbed Jenny by her long hair and hauled her to her feet. 'How's about you fixin' us something to eat, girl?'

Jenny sobbed loudly and started to pull on her tattered clothes.

Sutcliffe watched her go around the cabin in a daze as she prepared the food for them. Homer had gone outside and returned with a couple of chickens he had killed and plucked. There was silence in the cabin as the food was prepared for the men.

'Bes' give him some too,' Homer told the girl as he held her by the wrist and stroked her arm.

Sutcliffe watched her stumble into the kitchen to get the food. When it was ready, she brought it in a sullen silence and put it down in front of the men. The Morris boys were noisy eaters, and not too well versed in the way of good manners. Soon the table looked like a pigsty, with Jenny slowly working up, what appeared to Sutcliffe, powerful hatred.

'What ya lookin' at, girl?' snarled Ben, when he caught her staring at them. The girl turned and looked away.

Ben's fist caught her at the side of the head and sent her spinning across the room.

'Mighty fine of you,' Sutcliffe snarled at him, from the corner where he had been eating.

'Shut up, bounty man,' Ben spat at him.

'Why? You goin' to put a bullet in me?' Sutcliffe asked.

Storming across the room, Ben dragged him to his feet. Sutcliffe let the plate slip from his hands and fall to the floor. Wrapping his feet around Ben's legs he pulled them both over. They hit the wooden floor of the cabin, amid the laughter of the others, including Durrant. While they wrestled on the floor Sutcliffe let his hands move around Ben's waist until he found the bone hilt of the man's knife. Sliding it up out of its sheath, he slipped it under the sleeve of his shirt, then let Ben get the best of him.

He rode the pain inflicted by Ben's boots until Ben got tired of it. Sutcliffe figured it was worth the pain to have got hold of the knife.

Satisfied that he had taught the bounty hunter a lesson, Ben hitched up his belt and returned to the table. Watching him, Sutcliffe felt himself go cold, but it had been the best that he could think of. He only had to reach around to the back of his belt to discover that his knife was missing. Ben, however, was more interested in his food than anything else and went and sat down.

The girl sat huddled at the far side of the room, her back to them all while this was going on. Through one swollen, blackened eye, Sutcliffe looked at her, trying to figure out what was going on in her mind, but he could not. Homer got up from the table and started to search through the drawers.

'Hey, girl, your ol' man keep a bottle any place round here?' he barked at her.

Jenny made no sign of having heard him, and remained motionless, looking into space.

'You hear me, girl?' Homer caught her by the shoulder and got her to her feet. 'Said, did your ol' man keep a bottle any place round here?'

'Guess she's sulkin' at you, Brother,' Fred laughed from the table.

Rage crept into Homer's voice. 'You listenin' to me, girl?' he shouted, as he brought back his hand and slapped her across the face. Jenny's head went to one side with a force that Sutcliffe thought might break her neck. He saw a thin line of blood run from the corner of her mouth, down her jaw. Homer threw her to one side and continued his search until he found it.

'Time to tuck yer in fer the night,' Ben told him as he got up from the table with a length of rope in his hands. Sutcliffe braced himself and pushed the knife as far up his sleeve as he could.

The whiskey that they had been drinking started having its effect. When Homer tied the bounty-hunter's hands together he did not feel the knife, and he did not tie Sutcliffe's hands too tightly either. He lumbered back to the table and sat down to finish the bottle with the others.

As the night wore on, more and more glances were cast in Jenny's direction, and Sutcliffe began to fear that they would go at her again. He need not have worried, as, one after the other, their heads fell forward on to the table and they started to snore.

Darkness obscured almost everything in the cabin. Wriggling, Sutcliffe got the knife down his sleeve and into his hand. He sawed through the bonds as quickly as he could until the ropes parted.

'Jenny,' he called, as quietly as he could. 'Jenny, can you hear me?'

Receiving no answer, he catfooted across the floor until he reached the girl, who lay in the opposite corner, trembling violently.

'Leave me alone,' she said, as he put his arms on her shoulders.

'Listen to me, Jenny. I'm gonna git us out of here,' he whispered.

'No, you ain't. You're just gonna do what the others did to me, ain't you? Wish Pa was here. He'd fix you all.'

Sutcliffe clapped his hand over her mouth. 'Be quiet,' he told her. 'I don't want them awake yet.'

The girl had started to struggle and things were getting knocked over in the dark. Finally, Sutcliffe gave it up and let go of her mouth. She screamed loudly.

Taking a box of matches from his pocket, Sutcliffe got one to light. A lamp stood on the homemade sideboard. He lit it. The sudden flooding of the cabin with light brought the men at the table to their senses. Quickly, Sutcliffe disarmed them and tossed their guns into the night.

Scratching their heads and yawning, they looked at Sutcliffe with something like disbelief.

'Damn it, he's free,' Fred gulped, seeing Sutcliffe's Peacemaker levelled at them.

'Boy's got promise,' Sutcliffe said, with a cold smile.

'That he has,' Durrant put in.

'OK, Durrant, there's enough rope over there. Git 'em tied up.'

Once Durrant had secured the Morris brothers, Sutcliffe did the same for him.

'How are you feelin', girl?' Sutcliffe asked, putting his hands on Jenny's shoulders.

She twisted away and for the first time, he saw something deep in her eyes that worried him. She said nothing, but went to the far end of the cabin, a half-vacant look on her marked face.

'Why don't you go out an' make sure

them horses is saddled fer us?' Sutcliffe asked, as gently as he knew how.

'OK, Pa. I'll git the horses,' she said quietly, 'but watch that bounty hunter, he's one of them.'

Half-an-hour later they rode out.

* * *

Running Deer was impatient to get on. She felt that Somers and Brown were deliberately slowing things down and she knew what their motive was. Durrant had kept the hiding place of their takings a secret, known only to himself and Mellors. Running Deer guessed that they planned to let Sutcliffe get her man to Fort Smith and hand him over to the authorities. Then they could kill Mellors and Harkins, get the money and keep it for themselves. As they moved along the trail she tried hard to form a plan of her own. But for the time being she needed them both.

At noon, they halted. Somers and

Brown sat a little apart from the rest as White Elk prepared the food. They ate in silence for a moment, then Running Deer spoke quietly. 'Those two,' she said. 'I do not think we can trust them. I am not sure about Three Fingers.'

'You'd be plain right,' Mellors told her, to her surprise. 'Bart was gonna cut 'em loose, but this bounty man got in the way. Sure made a mess of things.' He pushed a piece of buffalo meat into his mouth.

'Then what shall we do?' Running Deer asked, sipping from the water in the tin mug she was holding.

For a moment, Mellors did not speak. Then he said, 'Way I see things, this *hombre* Sutcliffe's a tough piece of flesh. Brought in them Gomez boys single-handed a couple of years back. Bin doin' that kinda thing regular as clockwork ever since. Need their guns fer the time bein'.'

'And when we do not need their guns?' White Elk asked.

Mellors shrugged. 'When we don't need 'em, we don't need 'em.'

A look of satisfaction crossed Running Deer's face. 'That is good.'

Having finished eating, they mounted up again and moved out down the trail. The darkness had started to close in when Running Deer saw the cabin through the trees.

'It is strange,' she told Mellors, as they halted out of sight and dismounted. 'No light shows and there is no smoke from the cooking fire.'

Mellors scratched his chin thoughtfully. 'Runnin' Deer, you an' White Elk take a looksee. Me an' the boys'll cover you.'

White Elk gave him a surprised look, as he drew his revolver.

'Won't seem as suspicious if two women come down the trail instead of a bunch of men.'

The answer did not appear to appease White Elk, but there was nothing to be done about it. She and

Running Deer moved slowly towards the house. Behind them, Somers and the others watched their progress, guns drawn.

It did not take the two women long to return to where the others waited. 'They have been here,' Running Deer told them.

'How d'ya know it was them?' Mellors asked, putting his gun away.

'Bart scratched a mark on the table. A mark I would know if he ever got into trouble.' Running Deer fidgeted with the leathers of her horse.

'Turned out to be a damn good idea,' Three Fingers said with a laugh.

Running Deer swung on him. 'Be careful, Three Fingers, he is not dead yet.'

'Didn't mean no offence, Running Deer.' Three Fingers' tone did not hide his contempt for either Running Deer or Durrant.

'Running Deer don't take none, Three Fingers.' Somers stepped between them both. 'Now, let's get us some shelter.

Ain't no point pressin' on in the dark.'

They followed him into the yard. Inside, Running Deer and White Elk got the fire going and fixed food for them.

7

'Take a good long look at it, boys,' Sutcliffe told his captives with a note of triumph in his voice. 'In a couple of days, you'll be enjoying prison food. Got to admit I won't be sorry.'

'It's got to be better than this slop. Beginning to think yer might be tryin' to poison us. Save the court the price of keepin' us.' Durrant spat out the mouthful of bacon that Jenny had cooked for them, in silent protest.

Sutcliffe turned. The girl sat hunched over the fire, staring intently into the flames.

'Wouldn't have blamed her if she'd fed you slow poison for what you did to her.' Sutcliffe's hand gripped the edge of his plate; it took him all his self-control not to throw its contents over the outlaw.

'Sure gave us a good time back in

that cabin.' Homer dropped in his two cents' worth. 'Pity we ain't gonna git to do it again.'

Durrant and Homer's two brothers laughed. Sutcliffe dropped the plate and drew back his foot to plant it in Homer's face. Suddenly, he found his leg hooked from under him and the world turning cartwheels.

The four men scrambled to their feet and shoulder charged Sutcliffe as he got up. Four pairs of boots slammed into his body. Jenny gave a cry and jumped to her feet. Durrant slammed into her and sent her sprawling across the fire. Before she could get to her feet, Durrant put his foot in her face and pressed his weight down on it. She screamed again.

As the booted feet slammed into Sutcliffe's body, the three remaining outlaws struggled to get out of their bonds. But Sutcliffe knew that for these men it was a desperate make-or-break attempt and he fought back with everything he had. At last, sheer desperation gave him the upper hand and he managed to get to his feet. He shoulder charged his way out of the semi-circle and drew out the Peacemaker. A single shot into the air told the outlaws that for the time being it was all over.

'Back, git back,' he called out, his chest rising and falling with the effort of breathing. 'Durrant, git over here. Now.' He noticed the slight hesitation in Durrant's desire to move from his position astride the girl.

The men, breathing hard, stood with their backs to a tree.

'Go on, Pa, finish them off. They've bin asking fer it.' The outburst from behind him took him completely by surprise.

Still keeping his gun on the men, Sutcliffe turned. Jenny's mind had given way under the attacks by Durrant and the Morris brothers.

Sutcliffe tightened the bonds on the men's hands.

'Reckon I'm gonna have to feed yer

from now on,' he told them, as he finished tightening the ropes around Homer's wrists.

He looked across at the girl who was staring fixedly at the group. Her vacant eyes moved up to his face.

'You're one of them, ain't you?' The voice was harsh and strident. 'You think I don't know what you're up to, don't you?'

'I'm takin' these men to Fort Smith. Judge Parker'll hang 'em for what they did to you.' His mouth had become dry and he suddenly felt in need of a drink, whiskey for choice.

'Got yer hands full,' laughed Homer. 'If she thinks yer one of us, maybe you should untie us an' show her you are.' They all laughed together. Getting up, Sutcliffe went over to them. He grabbed Homer and his fist crashed into Homer's ribs like a sledgehammer. He pounded at him, until his arms ached, by which time Homer was screaming for him to stop.

Breathing hard, he flung Homer

down on the ground. As he did so, he heard a horse galloping away from the camp. He spun round as Jenny disappeared down the trail lashing the horse with the leathers for all she was worth.

'That's one of us yer don't have to worry about,' Durrant sneered.

Going to the edge of the trail, Sutcliffe waved and called for the girl to come back, but she was out of sight.

8

As she rode on in a blind panic, Jenny
could see it all now. They were in it
together; the men who had raped her
and the man called Sutcliffe who was
pretending to take them in. They'd
killed Pa and Yeller for the land.
That's what they wanted, the land.
It was good land, just outside Indian
Territory. Good crops would have
grown there. But now they wouldn't,
and all that hard work Pa had put into
it would be wasted. Worst of all, they
were going to get away with it.

But why should they, she thought
suddenly, reining in the horse. The
Winchester that Pa had taught her
to use was still slung in the saddle
holster, and that would mean, she
almost whooped with surprise, that
the box of shells would be in the
saddle-bag, the ones that she had

used yesterday afternoon when she was down by the river shooting something for the pot. Pa often let her go down to the river to get something for the pot when he had other chores to attend to.

She got down from the horse and tethered it to a tree. A quick check of the saddle-bags told her that the box of shells was still there. Her hands found a hunk of pemmican. Pulling it out of the saddle-bag she tore a chunk out of it with her teeth. She ate hungrily until she had devoured half the dried meat. Then, caution for tomorrow took hold, and she put the rest back.

No, she told herself. You ain't gonna get away with it. She took a long drink from the canteen and remounted.

With the fading light, she knew that she could do nothing until morning. Then she would find them and, one by one, finish them off.

★ ★ ★

Sutcliffe slept uneasily. Occasionally he woke himself up and checked his prisoners. They slept soundly, more soundly, he thought, than men facing a rope at Fort Smith ought to sleep.

The sun caught him already half-awake. Getting to his feet, he stretched stiffly. The four of them moved. He helped them up, applying his boot to their asses until they were fully awake.

They came awake cursing and swearing. Sutcliffe hunkered down and made fresh coffee. One by one, he unfastened their hands, despite what he had told them the night before. He allowed them a mug of coffee and some beans before fastening them up again. When he had done with them, he fed himself.

'Guess the little lady's miles from here by now,' Ben laughed quietly.

'Yer bein' a mite free with yer mouth,' Sutcliffe warned him. 'Wouldn't want yer missin' out on what Homer got,' he added.

'Reckon you'll be gettin' it back plus a bit extra,' Homer said with difficulty, the pain in his ribs not having subsided much from the beating that Sutcliffe had given him the night before.

'One thing's fer sure,' Sutcliffe said, having got them in their saddles and rounded on them. 'You cain't talk your way to Fort Smith.'

They started on down the trail.

★ ★ ★

Jenny had slept badly, her mind in a turmoil from the dreams that haunted her. She awoke looking hag-ridden, her hair a wild mess and her clothes and hands grubby.

Filling up the canteen from a nearby stream, she took a drink and a little more of the pemmican. Then she rode back the way she had come. It did not take long for her to find the place where she had run from them, and soon she was following their trail.

'What's eatin' you, Homer?' Durrant asked of the man next to him. 'Somethin' in yer shirt cain't keep still?'

Homer had been looking over his shoulder for the last ten minutes while straining at the ropes.

'Dunno,' he confessed. 'Things jus' don't feel right, that's all.' The stubble on his face was making it itch.

'Could be a combination of things,' Sutcliffe told him. 'Could be a guilty conscience, but I doubt it. More like yer beginning to feel that rope bitin' into yer neck.'

Jenny pushed aside a long branch and watched them. Homer Morris and Durrant were in front, with Fred and Ben riding just in front of Sutcliffe, who had his Winchester resting across the saddle bow.

She too had her Winchester, and she cocked it. Carefully, she raised it and lined up Ben in the sights. He had been the one to use her first, so it seemed only right that he should be the first one to die. As she took up the slack of the trigger ready for the shot, Sutcliffe moved between her and her target.

With a muffled curse of frustration, she lowered the rifle and pulled back into the undergrowth. Something prompted Sutcliffe to turn and look back down the trail. He could see nothing but the shadows caused by the sun.

With her first attempt frustrated, Jenny swung wide and moved through the undergrowth, her temper gradually settling. She moved on until she had come out on an unused trail. Rowelling her horse, she picked up speed, raising a cloud of dust.

Judging herself to be wide of the group and in front of it, she plunged once more into the undergrowth until she rejoined the trail that Sutcliffe and his party had taken.

Dismounting, she hitched the horse

to a branch and levered a round into the breech of the Winchester.

'Won't be long now, Pa, 'til I git the first one,' she muttered to herself, her eyes narrowing on the trail.

The time seemed to move slowly: then she saw them, a tightly clustered group with Fred in front, his hands behind him. The rifle came up to her chin seemingly of its own volition.

He rode with his head up, like he hadn't a care in the world. Once or twice he cast a glance at his companion. A thin line of sweat had broken out on his forehead. They were so close now that she could hear them talking and the jingling of the harness. Pushing up the Winchester against her shoulder, Jenny curled her finger around the trigger and held her breath as she squeezed it. The Winchester bucked and spat blood-red flame. Birds rose in a cloud from the trees.

Sutcliffe caught the flash of the sun on the metal of the Winchester a split second before Jenny squeezed the trigger. Even as he called out, the rifle shot echoed through the undergrowth. Fred's head jerked backwards, spraying blood and bone over Ben.

'What in hell?' called out Ben, as Fred fell back in the saddle, then toppled out of it altogether.

Sutcliffe hit the ground a second before Fred did, his eyes searching for a target. Grabbing Durrant by his coat, he pulled him out of the saddle and kicked him into the undergrowth. The others piled in on top of them.

'Murderin' bitch,' yelled Homer.

'Glad you know what it's like.' Sutcliffe's eyes scanned ahead, but could see nothing. 'Only person that's gonna grieve over it, is the hangman. Somebody's cheated him of a fee.'

Homer tried a kick of pure rage at Sutcliffe's head.

'You bastard, that was my brother,' he screamed.

'Move,' yelled Sutcliffe, elbowing him out of the way as he brought the rifle up to cover the trail.

Ahead of them, Jenny had pushed the Winchester into the saddle holster with a feeling of satisfaction. Swinging into the saddle, she urged it away from the scene of the ambush.

'I'm gonna — ' Homer started to say.

'Shut up, you damn fool,' Sutcliffe hissed. 'Whoever is out there sure knows how to use that rifle.'

Durrant gave Sutcliffe a sidelong look. He had been wondering who was up there and who was so good with that rifle. It had to be Somers. He licked his lips. Things were working out better than he had hoped.

Giving Homer and his brothers — well, brother — all that about splitting the take with them . . . He had known from the first that they'd be suckered in. Just didn't reckon on the boys getting here so fast.

'What are you sniggerin' at?' Sutcliffe's voice startled him.

'Nothin', bounty man, nothin','

Durrant looked away. 'We gonna stay here all day?'

'Don't reckon we'll have to,' Sutcliffe told him.

'How'd you figure that?' asked Ben, who was in cover behind a rock a few yards away.

'Thought I heard someone ride out just after the shot.' Sutcliffe looked carefully up the trail.

'You gonna find out?' Ben asked, encouragingly.

'No. You are. Just take a walk down that trail, an' stay where I can see you.' Sutcliffe waved the carbine in the direction of the trail.

Ben coloured up and then lost it when he saw that Sutcliffe meant what he had said.

'An' suppose I don't want to go.' His voice trembled as Sutcliffe levered one into the breech of the Winchester.

'Bullets don't cost much an' I got plenty more.' Baring his teeth, Sutcliffe gave a death's head grin.

His body trembling, Ben got to his

feet and gave Homer a last beseeching look.

'No good lookin' at him,' said Sutcliffe, and squeezed off a round at Ben's feet.

The outlaw danced to one side as the bullet kicked up dust within an inch of his foot.

'Don't worry. If I wuz goin' to hit you you'd be bleedin' all over the trail by now,' Sutcliffe spat in Ben's direction.

'Ain't you afraid that boy's gonna make a run for it?' Durrant asked, watching Ben.

'Wouldn't matter if he did. I could bring him down before he'd gone a yard.' Sutcliffe's eyes narrowed as he watched Ben lumbering down the trail. Every few yards he would turn and look in Sutcliffe's direction, but Sutcliffe just waved him on with the Winchester.

'See anythin'?' he called, just as Ben reached a bend in the trail.

'No.' The voice sounded dry and croaky.

'Seems I was right. Whoever took a shot at us must have taken off.' Sutcliffe got to his feet and motioned the others to do the same.

'Git in the middle of the trail where I can see you,' he said, as he backed towards the horses.

Gathering the leathers, he led the horses to where Durrant and the others waited.

'What about, Fred?' Homer asked. 'Ain't you gonna give us time to put him under?'

'Guess so. But you're gonna have to find something to dig a hole with, unless you got a shovel in your saddle-bag.' Sutcliffe was impatient to get on.

After Sutcliffe had untied his hands, Homer found the branch of a tree in the undergrowth. He broke it up and handed a piece to Ben who hacked at the ground with his piece. It took them a while, but in the end they had gouged out a hole big enough to drop Fred in.

'We want to say a few words.' Homer's voice was unsteady. For a moment Sutcliffe watched his face.

'Sure, as long as they're real short words,' he said coldly, remembering the men and women the Morris boys had put under without a word or a marker.

For a few moments there was silence as the Morris boys bowed their heads.

'OK, boys, time to be movin',' Sutcliffe said, when they were all back in the saddle.

As they started out again, he kept his eyes on the trail and the undergrowth. The only person he could figure was responsible for the shooting was Jenny. And he knew she was going to come at them again.

9

'Did real well, Pa.' Jenny sat with her back to a tree, taking bites out of the pemmican. She had been talking to her father for an hour, her mind having given way completely under the strain of the ordeal that the brothers and Durrant had put her through.

'Got him in the head. Just fell right out of the saddle.' She laughed loudly, then looked around.

'Yeah, you're right, Pa,' she said quickly. The clearing was still quiet, apart from the noise of the birds in the trees overhead. 'Don't want them catching up with us yet. Not 'til we got the last one. Gotta make them pay for what they did to us an' Yeller.'

After shooting Fred, Jenny had ridden like the devil, soon leaving them behind her. In the end, some common sense had caught up with her and she had reined in her horse to give it a breather, and had dismounted to rest.

For a while, she had closed her eyes and when she opened them she found her pa sitting across from her, with his same old weatherbeaten face, with the same old lopsided smile on it, and wearing the same old check shirt and brown trousers he had worn every day for years.

Confused, she closed her eyes again, but when she opened them, Pa had gone. It was getting that way with him. He'd come for a spell to chew the fat, then he'd disappear.

Jenny could see through the covering of trees that the sun was not far off its zenith. She decided that it was time to roust them again, try and get the one who had been riding just in front of the bounty hunter.

She thought about Sutcliffe. The deceitful one, she thought. All smooth words and 'How d'ya dos', but just like the other four, cold and heartless, just waiting to take his turn with her. Let him suffer a bit. One in the belly. Nice and slow; that way. He'd be a long time dying.

* * *

Sutcliffe had them strung out in front of him. They had been pretty quiet since Fred had taken the bullet in the head. Now, they were getting cautious, as though they sensed the approach of the girl. After they'd buried Fred, the brothers had a discussion and came to the same conclusion that he had: the girl was tracking them. Not Durrant. He had kept his mouth shut and said nothing. More than once, Sutcliffe wondered what kind of a snake was crawling through his mind.

They had come out of the forest and out on to the flat, open plain. Sutcliffe felt relieved when they left the cover of the trees behind them and were out in the open. He knew that the others would be as relieved as he was.

The girl had proved herself to be a good shot and endowed with an animal cunning, not to say vengeful spirit. Not that he blamed her for it; he felt he would have done the same if it had been him.

★ ★ ★

Somers went through to the kitchen where Running Deer was fixing coffee for them on the stove in the cabin. For a few minutes he watched her in silence. She was real good-looking for an Indian, and he'd been hankering after her for a spell.

'You're wasted on Durrant,' he told her, as he moved up behind her and put his arms quickly around her waist. Running Deer brought her foot down heavily on his instep. Somers gave a sharp cry of pain and staggered back, clutching as his foot.

'I am Durrant's woman,' she warned him, pointing the pot of steaming coffee in his direction.

'You may not have Durrant for much longer,' he said, dancing back out of range of the coffee.

'Whether I have him or not, he is more of a man than you are. And you will certainly never take his place,' she said angrily, raising the pot.

'We'll see about that when the time comes.' Somers gave an angry look and turned to see Mellors coming into the kitchen.

'What's all the commotion about?' Mellors was pulling his suspenders over his shoulders, his hair rough and tousled from sleep.

'Best go out there and find a trail,' Mellors said to Running Deer, when he got no answer. He took the pot from her. 'Be a pity to waste good coffee.'

With a scowl of displeasure, Running Deer went outside and led her horse out of the corral. She cantered down in the direction that the tracks were leading. She soon picked them up and knew that she would have no difficulty in following them.

Jenny had tied a piece of blanket round the stock of the rifle to cut down any reflection it might give off. She lay in a dried-out water-course, her horse down beside her. She had had no difficulty in finding the place where she had killed the first of them. It was even simpler to get within sight of them, then fade away and get up in front. Being no stranger to the plains, she knew the existence of the water-course. Her horse, a well-trained mare, allowed herself to be settled down on the ground in silence.

They were still a distance away when she caught sight of them. It seemed to take them a hell of a long time to reach her. As they got level, she levered a shell into the breech. Waiting until they were just passing her she aimed at Ben and squeezed the trigger. The Winchester blasted out once.

The impact of the bullet flung Ben out of the saddle and across the front of Sutcliffe's mount as Sutcliffe swung round to bring the Winchester to bear on the water-course. The horse panicked as it collided with Ben's body and reared up. The shock threw Sutcliffe's aim completely and the bullet from his Winchester went high over Jenny's head.

As soon as she had fired, Jenny scrambled to her feet, pulling her horse up with her. Jacking a fresh round into the breech, she pulled herself up on to the horse and wrapped the leathers around her hand.

With his horse under control, Sutcliffe fired at the retreating girl. She, in her turn, sent a bullet back his way. The bullet burned across his forearm causing him to drop the Winchester.

Falling sideways, Sutcliffe felt the cord holding Durrant's wrists looped over his own head and burning into his throat as it was tightened. He grabbed Durrant's wrists, pulling them both off the horses so that they hit the ground, knocking the breath out of their bodies.

A flurry of horses' hooves passed just wide of Sutcliffe's head as the cord around his throat bit tighter. The blood began to pound in his ears. He reached behind him and began to prise the hands loose from his throat.

'Give me a hand, you stupid bastard,' Durrant screamed, as he felt the pressure on his wrists tighten. Sutcliffe flung his head backwards and felt it smash into Durrant's face. Durrant screamed in rage and fury, and loosened his hold on Sutcliffe's throat.

Sutcliffe forced Durrant's wrists upwards until he had got them over his head. Homer was now out of the saddle and was hurtling towards Sutcliffe.

'Let it lay,' Sutcliffe's voice, and the sight of the bleeding figure holding a Peacemaker on him, froze Homer in his tracks.

'Take a step back.' Sutcliffe cocked the gun.

Homer backed off a step. Durrant rubbed his bloodstained face with his hands. 'You shoulda had him cold,' he told Homer angrily.

'With muh hands hog-tied? 'Sides you didn't do so great yourself,' Homer shouted back.

'OK, ladies, simmer down or I might shoot you now,' Sutcliffe laughed grimly.

Durrant and Homer did as they were told and moved away from the fallen Winchester.

'Now, let's git your asses on these horses,' Sutcliffe ordered them.

Sutcliffe turned in the direction in which Jenny had gone, but by now, she was out of sight. A warm trickle of blood reminded him of his wound. Tearing the shirt sleeve he inspected it. The wound hardly seemed worth the trouble of cleaning, being little more than a graze.

'Let's be movin',' he said, taking a look at his fast diminishing group of prisoners. He didn't want them all killed, otherwise there would be nobody to verify what had happened, and no money to claim.

'Your brother's gonna have to bury himself,' he said, as he touched the flank of his horse, addressing the back of Homer's head.

Turning angrily, Homer called out, 'Ain't you got a heart, Sutcliffe?'

'No, an' keep ridin',' came the unsympathetic reply.

This time Jenny did not ride far, only over the brow of the hill where she reined her horse.

Her maniacal laugh echoed over the silent landscape. She laughed again and again. Her once honey-blonde hair that had fallen to her shoulders hung matted, like rats' tails, her nails were broken and dirt was driven under them. Dirt had ground into her clothes.

'What's the matter, Pa?' she asked, when she settled down. 'Got him, didn't I? That bounty man cain't follow me for fear of losing them other fellas.'

10

'Just two more, Pa, an' the bounty man.' Finishing the water in the canteen, Jenny tossed it aside and wiped her mouth with the back of her hand. 'He's gonna be the one that suffers. Pretendin' to be all friendly-like, so them others could do it again. An' there's Yeller to think on.' At first, Jenny's voice had sounded reasonable and sensible, but it grew more strident with each word until it sounded more like shrewish scream.

Rising from the warm, dry grass, the girl paced up and down pulling at her lifeless hair, until she was running. Her eyes changed from blue, ice-cold chips to furnaces of burning coal, her claw-like hands beating at the stiflingly hot air. Her voice had become hoarse, the canteen of water having given out. Her tongue ran across her cracked lips.

Finally, arriving at her decision, she mounted the horse and headed after Sutcliffe.

The tired horse moved as best it could up the narrow gully. Impatiently, Jenny rowelled its flanks. She topped a rise and, abandoning her earlier caution, spurred her mount down the slope, pulling the rifle from its saddle holster.

Below, Sutcliffe and the others moved on obliviously. They had started to climb the hill when Durrant looked up. The sight of the galloping woman, her rifle raised to her shoulder, froze him in the saddle.

'Sutcliffe,' he yelled at the bounty man.

'What the hell's eatin' you?' Sutcliffe called out, but then saw what Durrant was seeing, his jaw wide, like a man facing retribution.

Taking in the situation, Sutcliffe made up his mind. It was time to settle with the girl once and for all. If she went on the way she was going, he'd be lucky to reach Fort Smith alive, let alone bring in a mess of prisoners, not that that bothered him. The girl was a good shot, but he wondered how she'd be with somebody shooting back at her and meaning it.

Pulling his Winchester from the saddle holster, he turned to Durrant and Homer. 'Sit tight, boys. I'll be right back.'

Homer and Durrant knew that if they ran for it, either the girl would get them or Sutcliffe would. Urging his horse forward, Sutcliffe rode full tilt at the oncoming girl. He brought the rifle up to his shoulder and squeezed off a round.

Jenny saw him coming, but paid him no mind, instead she loosed off a shot just as Sutcliffe fired. The distance between them was closing rapidly. Sutcliffe felt the rush of air pass his head.

Nothing seemed to happen, then the girl's horse started to fall. Behind him, he could hear the cry of triumph from

Homer and Durrant. From his rapidly moving horse, it seemed to Sutcliffe that Jenny had somehow kept the horse going, but then he saw that she had managed to slow it until she could jump from the saddle.

Rolling a couple of times, she got to her feet. By now, Sutcliffe was parallel with her. He reined in his horse.

'Put the rifle down,' he called to her. 'These men'll hang. Don't suppose Judge Parker'll be too hard on you fer what you did.'

Whether she heard him or not, he never knew for she had retrieved the fallen Winchester and was aiming it in his direction.

'Drop it,' he yelled, as he started to bring up his own gun. 'Drop it.' Sutcliffe gave her one last chance.

As she brought up the Winchester, he could see blood running down her arm.

Sutcliffe's rifle roared out. The girl staggered back, blood pumping from the top of her shoulder. Lowering the rifle, Sutcliffe glanced at the others. Durrant screamed something at him. He tore his gaze away from them back to the girl. Regaining her balance, she was slowly raising the rifle once more.

He knew then that he was going to have to kill her. He fired once more, aiming his shot at her heart. Jenny staggered back, the rifle slipping from her grip. She tottered once more then fell.

The whole prairie seemed to fall silent at this last act in the mad girl's tragic drama. Even Durrant and Homer were affected by what had happened. Touching his horse's flanks, Sutcliffe rode towards the fallen girl. Dismounting, he kicked away her rifle then bent down by her.

'Sorry, Pa,' she gasped. 'Thought I had 'em.'

A feeling of sorrow swept over Sutcliffe. 'You did damn well, Jenny,' he said quietly.

'Thanks, Pa,' she whispered, before closing her eyes for the last time.

Removing his hat, Sutcliffe stood in silence over the dead girl for a moment, then he looked up at the sky where the vultures were already wheeling.

'All right, you two,' he snapped at his prisoners. 'Git some rocks an' cover her up.'

'You let Ben lie, she can lie,' Homer answered.

Reaching up, Sutcliffe dragged him to the ground and laid the rifle across his head. Homer staggered away, his head bleeding, his mouth full of curses.

Looking up, Sutcliffe watched as Durrant got himself down. 'Won't git no sass from me,' he said, his voice trembling when he saw the look in Sutcliffe's eyes.

Following them, the bounty man waited in silence as they heaped stones over the girl's body. As they did so, Sutcliffe could not help noticing how she seemed to have changed. The madness had gone from her face and her hair seemed to have regained its colour.

When her body was covered with rocks, safe from coyotes and vultures, Sutcliffe stood in silence, his head bared.

'You can join me in a few words or not, it's up to you,' he told them quietly.

Neither of them replied.

11

Sol Greer saw them coming in at first light. White Elk, Running Deer, Rick Mellors and the rest of the boys.

'Hi,' he greeted them, as they dismounted and watered their horses.

'Hi, Sol,' Mellors said, guiding his horse's head into the trough.

'You missed him by a night or two,' Greer told them, deciding to say nothing about the shooting that had left him with a patient to care for.

'How was Bart?' Running Deer asked.

For a moment Greer considered the question. 'Looked like he'd bin in a fight. Reckon Sutcliffe musta worked him over just to keep him quiet.' He spat into the dust.

Running Deer cursed at this. 'Sutcliffe's going to die,' she said.

Greer did not mind. So long as they

paid up and went away without too much trouble he was not bothered.

'Sell us some grub?' Mellors asked.

'Sure can,' said the suddenly affable Greer, leading them into the trading post. He watched, mentally tallying it all up as they took what they wanted.

'Reckon we got it all, Sol,' Mellors said, filling the last gunny sack before they left.

He peeled off a couple of $50s and tossed them on to the counter.

'Bart'll be real appreciative,' he said, with a grin.

'Will you be staying here?' Running Deer asked White Elk once they were outside in the yard.

'I think so, my sister. An evil hand clutches at my heart,' she told her.

'Farewell,' White Elk said, as Running Deer gigged her horse out of the yard. Somehow White Elk did not think she would see her sister again.

* * *

Hardin had spent a considerable amount of time in pain, but Greer had given him a bottle of the best, just to keep him quiet until Durrant's gang had gone.

During the afternoon on which Sutcliffe had ridden out, Greer and another fella had held Hardin down on the counter while the blacksmith dug out the bullet. Hardin's screams scorched the air as the blacksmith cut round the hole until he had found the shell. By the time he had finished Hardin lay unconscious among the blood and mess on the counter.

Greer and Harvey Wellbeing, had carried the unconscious Hardin into the back room and put him on the pile of skins and sheets that the local whores used when trade got brisk.

'Soon git better now,' Greer had said, wiping his hands on a filthy piece of rag.

Hardin had been lucky. At first, he and Sutcliffe had figured that the bullet had smashed his shin bone; instead, it had missed by the fraction of an inch, tearing into the flesh.

'Guess he won't be on crutches fer long, if at all,' Harvey had said slopping out the room and sweeping the bloodied water outside.

'Means he kin git out after Sutcliffe, just in case Durrant's boys ain't as good as they think they are.' Greer threw the piece of rag on the counter and followed Harvey outside. They had both rolled quirlies and blew out the smoke towards the hills.

They waited outside, smoking, drinking warm beer, as they listened for the sounds that would tell them that Hardin was coming round. At last they heard the low moaning and the thrashing about as Hardin crawled out of the black pit into which the blacksmith's probings had sent him.

'Best git inside an' see how our patient is.' Greer's voice sounded heavy with sarcasm as he squashed out the quirly that was burning down to his lip. The blacksmith finished his beer, belched loudly, and followed Greer into the darkened room.

The thin face glowed with the sweat that ran down the thick stubble pushing through his flesh.

'How soon am I gonna be able to ride?' he demanded, when he saw the two men.

'Be no time at all.' Greer leaned against the wall, sipping at another glass of beer.

'Damn good thing too.' Hardin pushed himself up on his elbows and looked round the room. 'Where's my gun?'

'Y'ain't goin' anywhere, at least not fer a day or so,' Greer told him. 'That wound's gonna have to heal a mite. 'Sides, you know where you'll be able to find Sutcliffe.'

'It ain't just Sutcliffe I want,' Hardin told him. 'I want Durrant as well. Wuz countin' on makin' some big money outa his hide. Pass me some whiskey,' he added, rubbing his cracked lips.

In what passed for a bar, Greer got

a bottle of his best from beneath the counter and went back to Hardin.

'Harvey here says Sutcliffe's got two days on me,' Hardin said. Taking the bottle from Greer, he pulled out the cork and put the bottle to his lips.

'Got a mean thirst,' Harvey told him, as he watched the level in the bottle go down.

'What's it to you?' Hardin flared up. 'You payin' fer it or somethin'?'

Harvey backed off. 'Hell no, didn't mean nothin'. Just sayin'.'

'What wuz you jus' sayin'?' Once more Hardin tipped the bottle to his lips. 'Well?' he snarled, his eyes bright with whiskey and hot temper.

'Jus' sayin' nothin',' Harvey growled sullenly. 'Jus' if yer goin' after Sutcliffe yer gonna need more than Greer's best whiskey inside you.'

'Yeah, suppose so.' Hardin rubbed his belly after putting the bottle on the floor beside him. 'How about some grub?' he asked.

'Sure thing.' Greer spoke slowly,

working out how much he could screw out of Hardin for the food.

He came back half an hour later with a tray of freshly fried bacon and beans and a couple of eggs.

Hardin pushed himself up into a sitting position.

'Feel better already.' He rubbed his hands eagerly as he reached for the eating irons beside the plate.

'Feel like a shave an' a scoop over with some hot water,' said Hardin, as he pushed away the plate and looked meaningfully at Greer. Harvey had gone about his business.

'Water an' a razor.' Greer walked out, the empty plate balanced on his upturned fingers.

'Fix some hot water an' take it in there,' Greer told Michele, one of the post's whores who was leaning on the bar waiting for trade.

'Might miss a customer,' she told him with a sassy tone to her voice, as Greer came up to her with the plate.

Slamming it down, he caught Michele

by the shoulder and swung her round.

The copper-haired whore's face paled as Greer's dirty fingers dug into her flesh. 'Go and git that water fer him,' he told her, pushing her back towards the bar.

'Yeah, OK.' Michele glared at him as he went out to the yard.

Pouting, she went to the kitchen and prepared the water for Hardin.

'You're gonna look a sight different soon as you've got clear of that stubble you've got all over yer face,' she told him as she carried in the bowl of water along with the razor and soap.

Hardin paid her no mind, but took the stuff and started cleaning himself up.

Having washed his face, he used the razor, cutting down the stubble like wheat in a summer field. When he had finished, he ran his hand over his smooth face and called out for Greer, but Michele came into the room instead.

'Got the makings of a pretty fella,'

she told him, as she took the bowl.

'Nice of you to say so.' Hardin preened himself and looked around. 'Got a mirror?' he asked the waiting girl.

'Reckon I've got one upstairs.' With that, she went up to her room to get the small mirror she kept in her bag.

'Thought you'd gone to Fort Smith fer it,' Hardin said, as he held it to his face and examined his handiwork. There was only one cut on his face, just on the jaw, and that was not too deep.

'There's some folks round here that surely do admire themselves and not with much reason.' Michele smiled a little as she watched Hardin run his hand down the side of his face.

'Not a bad-lookin' piece of baggage, fer a whore,' he replied, and ran his eyes up and down the slim-figured girl.

'Sight more honest than huntin' men down fer money.' She turned and left Hardin smoothing his face and watching himself in the mirror.

When Michele had left the room, he pulled back the sheets. The bandage that Greer had tied round the wound was dirty and soiled, but it had prevented any further bleeding. The wound itself beneath the bandage burned a mite, but not as bad as Hardin had feared it would. Finding a clean piece of cloth, he cut himself a fresh bandage and rebound the wound.

Slowly and gingerly, he swung his feet over the edge of the blankets and got them down on to solid ground. Holding the edge of the table, he shuffled forward then let go of his support. For a second, he swayed and went dizzy, then the feeling passed and everything became normal again. For a few moments, he stood on his own account. The fire in his shins had subsided. Hardin wiped the line of sweat from his forehead and hobbled towards the door. Swinging himself round, he hobbled back again.

Outside, Michele found herself

thinking about the wounded man in the back room. He had good looks and the sense to say nothing that would have caused Sutcliffe to finish him off when he had him under his gun; the sort of man she had dreamed of for years. As she saw things, she would spend her life working in places like the trading post until she got too old for it, or some crazy customer cut her throat, like one of them had done for her ma. She mooned about, killing time until the customers started to come in.

'Hey, wake up, girl,' she heard Greer call to her.

Swinging her head round, she saw him at the far end of the room. 'C'mon, honey. You've got work to do.' He laughed loudly and slapped her ass as she went past.

Dragging herself back to reality, Michele made her way to the room where the customers waited.

Hardin hauled out his side gun and cleaned it. Closing the chamber, he spun it. The movement was free and easy. Dropping it back into the leather he limped out into the main room just in time to see Greer pointing the way for Michele.

The anger boiled up inside him and his leg started to burn. For a moment, he thought about going across and slapping Greer, but then as Michele disappeared into the other room, he reconsidered the matter. It was almost certain that he would have to kill Greer. That did not bother him unduly, he reckoned that he could outdraw the man, but Greer would have friends in the place who would take his side. So, instead of doing anything, he went back to his room and took the weight off his aching leg by lying down.

Apart from his sudden and growing fondness for Michele, something else troubled his mind. With every hour that passed, Sutcliffe and Durrant were getting further and further away. Come the morning, he knew, he would have to forget about the pair or go after them. His leg needed more rest, but a price of $5,000 hung over Durrant's head and Hardin knew that this would be his big chance, provided he could make it. Five thousand could buy him the old Jackson spread back where he came from and give him a good start.

The whore, Michele, looked to have a good body capable of bearing children. With any luck, he reckoned, he'd soon be in a position to give up this bounty-hunting business, provided he could plug Sutcliffe and get Durrant back to Fort Smith. He fell asleep thinking of the whore and the future.

The hot sun flooded in through the small window of the trading post as Michele came in carrying a tray of food for him.

'Hi,' he said, pushing himself up on the pillow.

'Hi yerself,' Michele told him, laying the tray across the bed. 'Looking a mite better this morning.'

'Feel even better if I had a kiss,' he laughed.

To his surprise, the girl cupped his

chin in her hands and pressed her lips to his.

'That's better than breakfast's gonna be,' he told her.

'Glad you think so,' she laughed.

Catching her wrist he pulled her towards him.

'You like to be here when I get back?' he asked her.

'Can't think of anywhere else I'd be goin',' she said miserably.

'I'm fixin' to buy a spread on the Brazos,' he said, as he cut up a piece of the steak.

'Nice part of the country. We'll talk about it when you get back,' she said seriously.

An hour later, after he had eaten and paid Greer, Hardin rode out of the trading post, with Michele standing on the veranda watching him go.

12

'Gonna face Judge Parker with a clear conscience.'

The three men were sitting by the trail while Sutcliffe cut some jerky for his prisoners.

'What's that supposed to mean?' Durrant took the food from the edge of Sutcliffe's knife with his teeth and commenced chewing. Sutcliffe had not untied them, nor would he until they reached Fort Smith.

'As I recall,' — Sutcliffe cut a second hunk and fed it to Homer — , 'part of the deal was to show those boys where you'd buried your heap an' ride out, free an' clear.'

'So?' Durrant swallowed.

'So how about tellin' me where it is? Cain't say it'll go any easier fer you with Judge Parker; there's still gonna be a rope at the end of it.' Sutcliffe cut himself a piece of the dried beef, and chewed into its leathery texture.

'Hogwash,' the outlaw laughed. 'I tell you that an' more than likely you'd put a bullet in the both of us. Say we'd made a break for it or some such, then collect your bounty an' spend my hard-earned loot.' He spat contemptuously. 'Fergit it, Sutcliffe.'

Sutcliffe sighed inwardly. He knew that would be Durrant's answer, but he had had to try. 'Let's git.' He wiped the edge of the knife on his trousers and pushed it into the sheath that hung from the back of his gunbelt.

* * *

Rick Mellors and Pete Somers weren't happy with the time they were making on Sutcliffe and Durrant. Somers was having another problem as well. Running Deer's threat with the coffee had just increased his desire for her, to such an extent that it was getting out of control, a mite like a forest fire.

129

It had to be put out or burn itself out. The squaw had taken a dislike to him right from the moment he'd joined the gang.

And the way things were going, he didn't think they'd catch up with Sutcliffe before he got Durrant to Fort Smith, and once Durrant was in Fort Smith, he wouldn't be coming out.

It was the end of the day and they had camped just off the trail. Three Fingers and Willy Brown were tending the horses, Rick Mellors had got a fire going and was fixing up some coffee. Somers had hunkered down beneath a tree. Running Deer walked past him, carrying the canteens to fill from a stream that ran a few yards away.

Somers watched her disappear down the trail. Mellors had his back to him, putting more wood on the fire. Somers decided that it was time to make his move. He catfooted to where Mellors was dropping a couple of lumps into the flames.

As Mellors turned to face him,

Somers quickly drew his pistol and brought it down on his pard's head. Rick Mellors slumped forward, blood flowing from the back of his head. Neither of the others had seen anything. Somers smiled and headed down the path that Running Deer had taken.

Running Deer had just filled the second canteen when her keen ears picked up the footfall behind her. She knew immediately from its sound that it was Somers. Rick would have called out. The others were very heavy-footed, like thirsty buffalo going for water. Unhurriedly she put the canteen down, replaced the stopper, then stood up slowly, turning to face Somers. She could see from the look on his lecherous face what he wanted.

'Rick's just got a fire goin'; the others won't be joinin' us for a spell,' he said, as his eyes ran over her body.

'Good,' she said. 'I do not think Rick would understand.' Running Deer spoke slowly, her hand moving towards the hunting knife she had hidden in her dress for just such a moment. She had always known that it would come and that Somers would be the one to bring it.

She let him get up close to her, his hands reaching out to put around her waist. Then she moved, quickly. She brought out the hunting knife and had the satisfaction of seeing the look of surprise and then fear on Somers' face a second before she drove it into his stomach.

Running Deer twisted the blade as the blood began to spurt out on to her hands. Somers gripped her hands fiercely and tried to twist them away from the knife. The squaw laughed and hung on as his convulsions increased. Then, with a whoop of joy, she gave the knife one final twist and let it slip through her fingers. His legs kicked for a moment and then became still.

With a jerk, Running Deer pulled the knife free and walked back to the others. The first thing she saw was Three Fingers and Willy Brown gathered around the still-stunned Rick Mellors.

Rick saw her first and tried to get to his feet, but the others pushed him back.

'Stay where you are,' Three Fingers said, probing the back of Rick's head, his fingers covered in blood.

'Where's Somers?' Rick asked her, struggling to his feet, despite the protest of the others.

'Down there,' Running Deer told him, jerking her thumb in the direction of the stream.

'What the hell's goin' on?' he demanded.

'He wanted something that was not his,' she told him. 'I have killed him,' she continued.

Three Fingers and Brown went off to see for themselves.

When they came back, they found Running Deer cleaning up the back of Mellors' head.

'Did a hell of a job on him,' Three Fingers said admiringly.

Running Deer bound up Mellors' head and gave him half a mug of whiskey.

'Should give him an even worse head in the morning,' Willy Brown laughed.

'Head or no head, we'd better be makin' up some ground in the mornin' or they'll have Bart hung before we can do anything about it,' Mellors said, nursing his head.

★ ★ ★

Despite his leg wound, Buz Hardin was coming up on them all pretty fast. During the day he had spared his horse nothing, pushing it to the limits of its speed and endurance, begrudging it every halt it needed. Now, as night fell and Mellors and Sutcliffe bedded down within a few miles of each other, he, too, lit a fire, examined his leg and brewed some fresh coffee. Despite the aching in his leg and the knowledge that he would have to face Sutcliffe before he could relieve him of his prisoner, the thought of the spread on the Brazos and Michele drove him on and haunted his dreams that night.

He woke and saddled up at roughly the same time as those he was pursuing and, like them, he had a quick breakfast and then headed out.

Again, he rode all day, but this time he sensed that the horse would need a less exhausting day, so he slowed it a mite and let it walk. After a spell, Hardin pulled his canteen from the saddle horn and put it to his lips. He was surprised to find it half empty. Draining it, he looked about him. Below him he saw a stream running through some trees.

He gigged his horse down into the small grove. The place was well shaded from the heat of the sun. Hauling on the horse's leathers, he climbed down and led the horse in the direction of the stream. As he walked, the ground fell a little way towards the water. At first, he did not notice it, then his eyes caught the burned-out fire and the flattened grass around it.

Hardin walked across to the mess and looked it over. Bending down, he quickly withdrew his hand; the embers were still hot, which meant that he was practically on top of them. Greer had told him that Durrant's gang were following Sutcliffe.

For a moment, Hardin thought about it. If he went tearing on at his present speed, he would like as not run straight into them. He grinned to himself. Why not let them fight it out between themselves then move in to pick up the pieces? Remembering his canteen, he walked down to the stream.

Hunkering down, he took the top off the canteen and laid it in the stream, so that the water could run into it. As he did so, the sun caught on something shiny in the grass. For a moment, Hardin stared at it. Then he got up slowly, ignoring the pain in his shin. As he approached it, he saw that it was a spur attached to a boot. A second later, he found himself looking down at Pete Somers' face.

Hardin almost whooped with joy. White Elk had stayed at Greer's place, but she was no account, being a woman, Somers was lying in front of him. Things were starting to come out just fine. He limped back to his horse and painfully got aboard.

★ ★ ★

'Cain't be that far ahead now, boys,' Mellors told those behind him. 'Best take it a little more carefully, don't want to spook Sutcliffe into letting the boss have it.'

They moved on carefully, their eyes peeled for any movement on the prairie.

'Got 'em,' Three Fingers sang out, pointing to a faint movement on the horizon.

Running Deer's heart leapt. She would soon be reunited with Durrant, and Sutcliffe would be dead.

'There's three of 'em,' Three Fingers said.

'Sure is,' Willy Brown affirmed.

'OK,' said Mellors, who had been doing some quick thinking. 'Running Deer, you and Three Fingers swing out wide. Get ahead of 'em and keep 'em pinned down, while me and Willy come up behind 'em.'

'As you say.' Running Deer hauled her horse out of the line and, followed by Three Fingers, set off at a steady lope out to the right flank.

Mellors and Willy Brown checked their guns and moved cautiously out towards the trio.

* * *

Durrant felt something behind him, he turned slowly so as not to arouse Sutcliffe's suspicions or give any warning to Homer. For the last hour or so, he had been starting to worry. Back a-ways when Jenny had come after them, he had been convinced that it was Rick and Pete.

The boys had not shown and Fort Smith was less than two days' ride away. He licked his lips. Unless they showed up soon, Sutcliffe was going to have his way and he was going to hang.

The morning dragged on with Running Deer and Three Fingers skirting Sutcliffe and pushing on ahead to the rocks they had seen and which would give them cover from which to shoot down Sutcliffe. Rick Mellors and Willy Brown stayed behind.

The sun was directly overhead when Sutcliffe thought he saw it catching on something in the distance. A moment later, a bullet from a Winchester took off half of Homer's head. He gave out one scream as hair and skull mixed in with blood showered over Durrant.

Flinging himself out of the saddle, Durrant rolled into the cover of a gully with Sutcliffe landing on top of him.

'Looks like yer boys have arrived,

Durrant,' he said, levering a round into the breech of the Winchester he had hauled from his saddle boot.

'Cut it a mite fine fer my likin',' Durrant complained ungratefully.

'Don't let it worry you, you ain't out of it yet.' Sutcliffe threw a slug in the direction of the rocks from where he had seen the reflection. The bullet struck the rock and threw up some dust.

'Throw yer gun out an' you can walk away from this,' Durrant told him magnanimously.

'Can't see it myself. I'd always be on yer tail, and you know it,' Sutcliffe told him.

'Seemed like somethin' worth tryin',' Durrant replied pressing himself closer into the ground.

Another bullet pitched into the dust in front of Sutcliffe's face.

'Tryin' real hard your boys, I'll give 'em that.' Sutcliffe returned the bullet along with two more.

'A fair way of getting rid of your

ammunition,' Durrant gloated.

Sutcliffe did not like to agree with Durrant, but unless he got lucky soon all he would have left was the ammunition for the Peacemaker, and that would not reach the rocks.

Above him, the sun was getting hotter and hotter. The horses had strayed a little with the canteens on their saddle horns. Gauging the distance, Sutcliffe knew that he would be dead before he got a yard.

'Heat gettin' to you yet?' Three Fingers called out from the shelter of the rocks.

'If it is, it's gettin' to yer boss as well,' Sutcliffe called back. A moment later, two more rounds kicked up dust a few feet away.

'Heat gettin' to you boys?' Sutcliffe mimicked Three Fingers' voice.

'Leave him, Three Fingers. He's trying to make you angry,' Running Deer told her companion.

'Sure succeedin',' Three Fingers told her. He picked up the canteen and took a drink, then he handed it to Running Deer.

The silence fell on the two groups.

Sutcliffe looked at Durrant. The outlaw dozed in the sun, seemingly unperturbed by the whole thing. Sutcliffe himself yawned and felt his eyelids droop. Then the bullet sang out just over his head. Immediately, his eyes opened. Another bullet ploughed into the ground.

'Where'd that come from?' he shouted.

'Sounds like I got some more help,' laughed Durrant.

Sutcliffe cursed. Now, he was hemmed in on two sides. He swore savagely.

From behind a rock, Mellors lined up the spot where he reckoned Sutcliffe to be.

'Why not call it a day, Sutcliffe? You've done yer best. Like I said, toss out yer gun and you can walk away from this mess,' Durrant said, chewing on a twig that he had found.

'And live about ten minutes? Decent of you to offer, though,' Sutcliffe said, his eyes still scanning the rocks. Then he saw it again. A flash of light, but not, he reckoned, the flash from the stock of a rifle, but from a mirror. He guessed Running Deer must be with them and it would have been her idea to use a mirror to signal to the others. Probably Mellors had signalled her first to tell her that he had arrived. Sutcliffe had known the Apaches to use this method of communication.

* * *

Buz Hardin had also seen the flash of light and guessed that Mellors had caught up with Sutcliffe and somehow roped him into some kind of trap. Having tethered his horse to some scrub, Hardin took his Winchester and crawled up the back of a rock. Lying flat, he could make out two figures in a dried-up wash.

Beyond, he could see a gully, and reckoned that Durrant and Sutcliffe were holed up there. Running Deer and the other man must be out in the rock up ahead.

Raising his rifle, he sighted Willy Brown's spine and squeezed off a round. Willy jumped when the bullet hit him, his rifle flying from his hands. Mellors, who had been lining up the gully for another shot, swung his head around and looked in the direction from which the shot had come.

'What the hell?' he babbled, as another shot took a lump of flesh out of his arm. He jumped up, then threw himself flat rolling out of the line of the third shot. Sutcliffe had a fleeting glimpse of Mellors and squeezed off a round, which went just wide.

'Don't know who's out there, but if your pals want to throw their guns out I don't mind,' he said to Durrant.

'The hell with you, Sutcliffe,' Durrant snarled.

An uneasy silence fell on the two camps.

Running Deer searched the ground below her. To the left of her and Three

Fingers, stood a cluster of rocks that flanked Sutcliffe's position. If Three Fingers could cross the open ground from their position, they would have Sutcliffe covered from three sides. If Rick could keep whoever had him pinned down occupied, it would be just a matter of time before they picked Sutcliffe off.

'Three Fingers,' she hissed.

'Yeah, Running Deer,' he answered.

Quickly, she explained her plan.

'Sounds fine to me,' Three Fingers told her, checking the ammunition in the Winchester.

Running Deer nodded to him and, as he started down the slope, she opened fire on Sutcliffe's position. Three Fingers threw the occasional unsighted shot as well, just to worry Sutcliffe.

Having seen him start his run, Sutcliffe threw some lead in Three Fingers' direction, but Running Deer's fire soon forced him to keep his head down. Three Fingers reached the rock and lined up on Sutcliffe's position.

Soon the lead was coming in pretty thick and fast, and Sutcliffe was having a hard time just throwing one back.

'Just a matter of time, Sutcliffe,' Durrant said, pushing himself further into the ground, so as not to be hit by the incoming fire.

From his position, Hardin was having an equally hard time with Mellors' fire, but was still able to get in a couple of close shots.

Sutcliffe wiped the sweat out of his eyes and filled up the Winchester with his last handful of shells. Durrant lay face down in the sand. Swiftly, Sutcliffe brought the Winchester crashing down on his head.

Sutcliffe dropped back into the gully and waited for a few more shots to come swinging in. He threw up his hands and cried out, then fell to the dust.

Above him, Running Deer had seen what had occurred. She stood up to shout a warning to Three Fingers, but

Three Fingers, who had seen Sutcliffe fall, let out a cry of triumph and ran into the open, with the intention of making quite sure Sutcliffe was dead.

Sutcliffe watched him come, but still did not move. He watched until Three Fingers was within yards of him, then he swiftly got to his feet and drew his Peacemaker.

Three Fingers froze in mid-stride and tried to bring the rifle to bear on Sutcliffe, but Sutcliffe already had his pistol in his hand, his finger curling round the trigger. The Peacemaker barked once and Three Fingers clutched his chest as the force of the bullet flung him backwards.

Running Deer's shot went just wide, and Sutcliffe was once more out of sight. Hardin and Mellors had seen what had happened, and once more there was a lull in the firing.

It's a stand off, thought Sutcliffe. They can't come in, we can't get out. Pity I don't know who's out there backing me. Unless it's that fool,

Hardin. Yeah, it's got to be him. Wonder just how much savvy he has?

A movement by his side attracted Sutcliffe's attention. Durrant had started slowly to come round.

Putting his foot on Durrant's back, Sutcliffe said, 'Keep still, Durrant, I just figured out a use for you.'

He looked up quickly for any sign of movement where Running Deer was holed up. A few yards away, the horses had started to drift in his direction. Now it all depended on how much savvy Hardin had. Grabbing Durrant by the scruff of his shirt collar, he dragged him to his feet.

'What the hell are you doin',' squawked Durrant. 'Yer just settin' me up. An' Running Deer misses me, you'll be next in line. An' what about Mellors? Fergit about him?'

Pushing the Winchester against Durrant's neck, Sutcliffe dragged him out of the gully and headed for the horses.

'Well? You hear me?' Durrant shouted.

'I ain't fergot about Mellors. I'm just hopin's that whoever's out there can take care of him — if he shows his ugly head,' Sutcliffe told him.

'You're crazy.' The sweat was pouring from the back of Durrant's neck.

They were out in the open.

'OK, Runnin' Deer,' Sutcliffe called out. 'Yer boyfriend's comin' with me. If yer gonna be shootin', best make it good.'

Seeing the movement below, Hardin prepared himself for whatever might come next. Moving away from the gully, Sutcliffe and Durrant went towards the horses. As they did so, Hardin saw Mellors rise to take a shot at Sutcliffe's back. He blasted out and hit Mellors' Winchester, the force of the bullet tearing the rifle from Mellors' hands. Hardin heard the cry of surprise and pain.

Running Deer was still looking for a shot when Hardin blasted Mellors' Winchester. When this happened she lowered her own gun, knowing she could not guarantee hitting Sutcliffe without running the risk of hitting Durrant.

'Nearly there,' Sutcliffe whispered in Durrant's ear.

'To hell with you, Sutcliffe.' Durrant's voice shook with anger.

Sutcliffe guided him between the horses, so that they were shielded from Running Deer and Mellors.

'Keep walkin'.' Sutcliffe caught hold of the stirrup of his horse.

They walked on awkwardly, still between the two horses.

Mellors and Running Deer, from their respective vantage points, watched with growing frustration until the two men mounted up and Sutcliffe headed them out.

Hardin watched what was going on below him. As Sutcliffe got Durrant into the saddle, he slid down the rock and got aboard his own horse, his aim to swing wide of Sutcliffe and his prisoner while keeping an eye open for Mellors and Running Deer. The way he figured it, he could pick up the pieces when Mellors caught up with Sutcliffe. It was just a matter of biding his time.

Running Deer came up out of the gully and found her horse. Mellors had done the same and was heading out to meet her.

'Couldn't fire again fer fear of hittin' Bart,' he told her.

'Neither could I,' the girl said.

'Cain't figure out who was behind me, put that bullet into Three Fingers. Sutcliffe don't work with anybody, so maybe it's someone tryin' to get in on the act.' His eyes roved the back trail.

'It does not matter. I think our paths will cross again. As for now, we must catch up with Sutcliffe before he gets to Fort Smith.'

They moved out cautiously, just within eyeglass distance of Hardin. Folding up the glass, he slipped it into his saddle-bag, and gigged his horse forward. He figured it would take them the rest of the day and part of tomorrow to reach Fort Smith. Above him, Hardin could see the sun starting to paint the sky a bloody red. He did not think that the others would risk trying to catch up with Sutcliffe in case they missed them in the dark and overshot them, which would mean that they would have to back track and risk missing them again.

'You gonna keep goin' all night?' Durrant whined as the light finally went.

'Why? You feelin' in need of yer beauty sleep, my murderin' friend?' The same thought that had gone through Hardin's mind went through Sutcliffe's. He had debated whether or not to push on hard to Fort Smith, but in the end had decided against it. The horses they were riding had not had a decent rest for some time and he himself was in need of some sleep.

Once they had got off the trail, he pulled Durrant off his horse and tied him to a tree.

'Now what are you figgerin' to

do?' Durrant asked, watching Sutcliffe gathering a heap of wood and laying it for a fire. Soon, it was blazing and Sutcliffe had fixed some coffee. He fed some of it to Durrant. Then, he cut up some dried meat, all the time making sure that the fire was pretty high.

'Don't know what yer doin' Sutcliffe, but they're gonna see that fire fer miles . . . ' Durrant stopped abruptly, the words dying in his mouth.

'Seems you got it right,' Sutcliffe told him, looking across the fire at him, his face an unearthly sight, with its thick stubble and days of trail dust illuminated by the dancing flames.

'Yer usin' me as bait, ain't you?' Durrant snarled.

'Why not? You've bin using other people, stealin' their money an' their cattle, along with their women. This is what I call justice. Seems fair to me,' Sutcliffe finished with a grim smile.

He got up, taking his bandanna from around his neck and gagged Durrant with it; then, for the second time that day, he slugged the protesting outlaw, who fell forward with a groan.

Taking the rifle from his saddle boot, Sutcliffe laid it at one side then stuck his hat on top of the saddle. Placing some logs on the ground, he stretched his blanket over them. He gave the place one last look, before gathering up his rifle.

'Be seein' you an' yer friends,' he said to the silent Durrant.

The fire made quite a blaze against the evening sky. Running Deer and Mellors saw it just as they were going to bed down for the night, intending to catch up with their quarry at first light.

'What d'you reckon to it?' Mellors asked of Running Deer, as they watched the glow against the sky. 'Reckon we should mosey up an' do somethin' about gettin' Bart back?' Mellors cut himself a hunk of dried meat and fed it into his mouth.

'Yes, but slowly. Sutcliffe is not a fool. There must be some reason for him lighting a fire like that,' Running Deer told her companion.

'Waal, if he's trying to sucker us in, maybe we'd best oblige.' Mellors smiled.

As they approached, the flames from Sutcliffe's fire grew. They moved up until they could see where Durrant was tied. Then, Running Deer saw the hat on the saddle, just as Mellors raised the Winchester.

'Wait,' Running Deer told him, putting her hand up to lower the rifle.

'Yeah, Mellors, you just wait a second.' The muzzle of Sutcliffe's Winchester touched the back of Mellors' neck.

'Drop the gun and git up nice and easy,' Sutcliffe told them.

He took a step back as they got up.

'Now, git yer hands up and head towards the fire,' he said, and prodded them in the back with the rifle.

They stepped slowly into the circle of the fire-light.

Giving a little cry, Running Deer tried to rush to the slumped Durrant, but Sutcliffe's harsh voice stopped her.

'Have you killed him?' asked the squaw.

'No, jus' been using him fer bait. Seems it worked, too.' Sutcliffe pulled Mellors' gun from its holster and tossed it to the ground.

'Your turn now, Sutcliffe.' Hardin's voice surprised them all. 'Come on, Sutcliffe, lay it down. I ain't got all day,' he said.

The rifle slipped through Sutcliffe's fingers and landed at his feet.

'Now what?' he asked.

For a moment there was silence and Sutcliffe had the idea that Hardin had not thought that far ahead.

The knife Running Deer had used to kill Somers flicked viciously through the night air.

'Look out, Hardin,' Sutcliffe shouted his warning. He threw himself clear. The knife struck Hardin high up in the arm. Mellors dived to retrieve his own gun, but Sutcliffe's boot caught him in the face and flung him backwards. Hardin fired at Running Deer, but his shot went high, and Running Deer took to her heels and disappeared into the brush, Sutcliffe taking off after her.

She headed for the trees where she and Mellors had left the horses. From the saddle holster she grabbed her Winchester, and started to circle back towards the fire, listening intently for Sutcliffe.

Mellors got to his feet and picked up Running Deer's knife that Hardin had pulled from his shoulder and dropped to the ground. Grabbing it, he headed for Durrant, who had just started to come round.

'Come on,' he yelled, hauling Durrant to his feet.

'That's as far as yer goin'.' Hardin's voice shook as the pain burned through his arm.

He had managed to get upright, and had his gun in his hand.

Mellors, who had been sawing through Durrant's bonds, pushed Durrant away to give himself room to draw, but Hardin cut him down. Then, he staggered back and lost consciousness.

13

Running Deer could see Sutcliffe just ahead of her. Slowly, she started to raise the rifle to shoulder level. Something warned Sutcliffe of the danger. Turning quickly, he raised the Peacemaker.

'Drop it, Running Deer,' he yelled.

Running Deer continued to raise the rifle and Sutcliffe's gun barked once. Running Deer spun away, the rifle falling from her grasp. Dropping his gun back into leather, Sutcliffe went over to her. For a moment, he wondered what she had seen in Durrant, then gave it up. Durrant staggered out of the undergrowth, his face a mask of rage and hate, a gun in his hand.

'You murderin' bastard, Sutcliffe, she's dead,' he screamed, and advanced on the wounded bounty hunter.

'She had her chance,' Sutcliffe told him.

'No rush is there, Sutcliffe? One in the leg for a start. Then the belly.' His finger tightened around the trigger, the gun barked and almost immediately Sutcliffe felt the burning pain in his thigh. His leg buckled under him and he went down.

'Damn you, Sutcliffe,' Durrant screamed, raising the gun once more. 'I loved her.'

Sutcliffe licked his lips and braced himself for the killing shot.

'Durrant,' Hardin called out, coming out from the cover of the trees.

Durrant turned to see Hardin holding a gun.

'Drop it, Durrant. Judge Parker don't like bein' kept waitin'.' Hardin swayed on his feet and Sutcliffe saw the blood streaming down his shirt.

Sutcliffe watched as Durrant lowered his arm, then suddenly raised it. Both of them fired at the same second. Durrant staggered back, the gun falling from his grasp. Then, suddenly, Hardin let his own gun drop and he fell to the ground.

Slowly, Sutcliffe pulled himself up again and staggered over to him. Hardin lay on his back, blood oozing from his shoulder wound.

'Ya promised me you'd kill me if you set eyes on me again,' he coughed, as he looked up into Sutcliffe's cold eyes.

Sutcliffe sighed. 'That sure seems to have been a long time ago,' he said.

'Waal?' Hardin called out to him.

'Sure in a hurry to meet yer Maker,' Sutcliffe's eyes closed on those of the wounded man. 'Ain't figured it out yet?'

'Figured what out?' Hardin's eyes filled with rage and anger. 'What's there to figure out? Either you're gonna kill me or you ain't. Which is it?' There was no pleading in the man's voice, he just wanted an answer.

'Sure I promised to kill you.' Sutcliffe had put the Peacemaker away and was rolling himself a quirly. He lit it and blew out that first lungful, then he hunkered down and offered it to Hardin, who took it a mite mistrustfully.

'What's your game, Sutcliffe? You the kinda fella that likes pullin' the wings off flies?' He blew out the smoke.

'Hell, no. I ain't got nothin' against flies. No more than the next fella. I've just been doin' some thinkin' out there.' He tossed a look in the direction from which they had come.

'An' what you bin thinkin'?' Hardin studied the bounty-hunter's face.

'Thinkin' about you and your partner — fergit his name.'

'Wuz Al Watkins,' Hardin grimaced through the pain.

'Yeah, that was him. But he doesn't matter now, he's dead.' Sutcliffe got to his feet.

'Like I'm soon gonna be.' Hardin rubbed his shoulder.

'Partner musta been damn glad to git away from you, you mournful bastard.'

Sutcliffe gave Hardin a sour look.

'Jus' keep on talkin' Sutcliffe, an' save yerself a bullet. I'm gonna bleed to death.' Hardin had prepared himself for it.

'Bin thinkin' about this money I got comin' fer Durrant's hide.' Sutcliffe threw the quirly away. 'I don't mind takin' money fer any man I killed, but I've been thinkin' on what they did to that girl — Jenny. An' it don't seem right to take money for killin' Durrant.' He spat out the name.

'So?' Hardin asked him, wondering what was going through the bounty-hunter's mind.

Sutcliffe turned to face him. 'What are you goin' to do now — if I don't kill you?'

Hardin licked his dry lips as he thought he might have a chance. 'Met this whore, Michele, down at Greer's place. Kinda took a shine to her. Think she kinda took a shine to me. So I figured goin' back that way with the money an' kinda marryin' up with

163

her. There's an old spread down on the Brazos. Gonna buy it up an' raise a few head of cattle an' a few kids. Sure as hell beats this fer makin' a buck.'

'Yer sure as hell right there; yer no damn good at this line of work,' Sutcliffe told him as he bent down and looked at the shoulder. 'Best git out while you've still got yer hide.'

'Man you ain't gonna kill me?' Hardin's voice was strong with relief.

'No. We're gonna go into Fort Smith an' you can claim the reward fer bringin' Durrant to a bad end.' He got his arm under Hardin's good shoulder and helped him to his feet.

'Then yer gonna git out of this line of work, marry yer whore, an' take up ranchin'. An' I sure hope you're better at raisin' kids an' cattle than you are at huntin' men. An' I'm sick of it. What happened to Jenny finished me with this line of work. Best thing we can do is git you that spread on the Brazos an' you raise the kids an' I'll raise the cattle.'

'Sounds fine to me,' Buz said gratefully.

THE END

We do hope that you have enjoyed reading this large print book.

Did you know that all of our titles are available for purchase?

We publish a wide range of high quality large print books including:
Romances, Mysteries, Classics, General Fiction, Non Fiction and Westerns.

Special interest titles available in large print are:
The Little Oxford Dictionary Music Book, Song Book Hymn Book, Service Book

Also available from us courtesy of Oxford University Press:
Young Readers' Dictionary (large print edition) Young Readers' Thesaurus (large print edition)

For further information or a free brochure, please contact us at:
Ulverscroft Large Print Books Ltd., The Green, Bradgate Road, Anstey, Leicester, LE7 7FU, England. Tel: (00 44) **0116 236 4325 Fax:** (00 44) **0116 234 0205**

US Marshal Luther Killeen is working undercover as a Texan pistolero in Tucson to find proof that the San Pedro Ring, an Arizona trading and freighting business concern, is supplying arms to the bronco Apache in the territory. But the fat is truly in the fire when his real identity is discovered. Clelland Singer, the ruthless boss of the Ring, hires a professional killer, part-Sioux Louis Merlain, to hunt down Luther. Now it is a case of kill or be killed.

GOING STRAIGHT IN FRISBEE

Marshall Grover

Max and Newt were small-time thieves, a couple of unknowns, until the crazy accident that won them a reputation and a chance to reform. But going straight in a town like Frisbee was not so easy. Two tough Texans were wise to them and, when gold was discovered in that region, Frisbee boomed and a rogue-pack moved in to prey on prospectors. In the cold light of dawn, the no-accounts marched forth to die.

TRAIL OF THE CIRCLE STAR

Lee Martin

Finding his cousin, friend, and mentor, Marshal Bob Harrington, hanging dead from a cottonwood tree is a cruel blow for Deputy U.S. Marshal Hank Darringer. He'd like nothing better than to exact a bitter and swift revenge, but as a lawman he knows he must haul the murderers to justice — legally. But seeking justice is tougher than obstructing it in Prospect, Colorado. Hank has to keep one hand on his gun and one eye on his back.

McKINNEY'S REVENGE

Mike Stotter

When ranch-hand Thadius McKinney finds his newly-wedded wife in the arms of his boss, the powerful, land-hungry Aaron Wyatt, something inside him snaps. Two gunblasts later, McKinney is forced to flee into the night with the beef-baron's thugs hot on his trail, baying for his blood. A man cannot run forever, and even when his back-trail is littered with bodies, the fighting isn't over. McKinney decides it is time for Wyatt to pay the Devil.